Hell's Canyon

Hell's Canyon

JOHN HUNT

A Black Horse Western

ROBERT HALE · LONDON

ISBN 0 7090 6218 4

Robert Hale Limited
Clerkenwell House
Clerkenwell Green
London EC1R 0HT

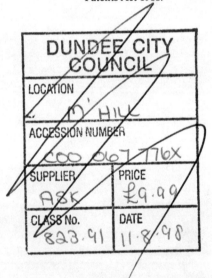

Photoset in North Wales by
Derek Doyle & Associates, Mold, Flintshire.
Printed and bound in Great Britain by
WBC Book Manufacturers Limited, Bridgend.

1

The Hellsville Country

It was a wide canyon with an abundance of the only genuine requirement for life – water – whose source was a confluence of several high-country creeks. Because water flowed downhill, the residents of Hell's Canyon, since prehistoric times, had used it to create a world flanked by forbiddingly forested highlands on three sides, north, east and west. Southward, the canyon was open for almost a half-mile made that way by capricious ancient winter flooding by the creek.

Succeeding generations had farmed the same fields, built on top of earlier villages, hunted the uplands and been isolated from the turmoil of the southward-lying open grasslands.

The nearest town was a settlement called Angelina whose name derived from an alleged saintly visitation 200 years earlier.

That visitation had resulted in legends of miracles that had been enhanced by passing generations. It could fairly be said that the territory of New Mexico probably had more legends, which *gringos* called superstitions, than most other territories.

It helped that in this area there were Indian beliefs, which, over the generations, could be found to parallel the native Mexican beliefs.

The inhabitants of Hell's Canyon were almost exclusively *norteamericanos* – *gringos*. The black-eyed natives had avoided the canyon since a priest named Alberto Lazaro had almost died there and, after a long recovery, had said his ailment had been the result of a holy man going into the canyon which of a certainty was the home of *fantasmas*, evil spirits, who not only haunted the place but who harried living creatures who trespassed into their secret world.

Harold Foster, the army doctor, who took up residence in Angelina after twenty years with the army, told Clyde Sotherland, also a resident of Angelina who was by trade a freighter, that Father Lazaro's ailment had been caused when the holy man had sat on a stump in the canyon where a centipede had been sunning itself. Father Alberto said the place was *Cañon de Inferno* – Hell's Canyon. What it had been called before the priest was attacked by evil ones went through a number of unpronounceable Indian names.

Some unregenerate *gringo* settler in the canyon, had opened a store around which several businesses now operated and because even isolated small hamlets should have a name, the original store-keeper had called it Hellsville.

The merchant had been dead almost thirty years. His store had passed through several owners. The current proprietor was what was called a 'black Irish'. His name was Rufus Malone. In colouring he could have passed as either a Mexican or an Indian.

He was a bull-necked individual of slightly less than average height whose weight could have been estimated at close to 200 pounds. It was said he had once lifted a full grown steer and if that were true or not it made an excellent legend and inspired a lot of respect.

Rufus Malone was unmarried. At least he had arrived in the canyon alone. He had a sense of humour that equalled his temper and in his own way was a private individual.

Hellsville would not qualify as a village, certainly not as a town. It would strain the appellation to call it a hamlet. Aside from the Irishman's general store, which was reasonably well stocked for the area, there was a leather works, and a café owned by a widow woman named Beulah Bell.

The canyon's soil was deep and rich. The biggest growers farmed about 200 acres. There were at least a dozen who farmed no more than ten to twenty acres.

Serious shoppers made the seven-mile trip to Angelina which had two rows of stores on each side of the broad main thoroughfare and that didn't count *la placita*, 'the plaza' in Mex town which was the original settlement and was very old. Aside from the *cantina*, Mex town had several businesses for the native trade. The *mayór* in Mex town was an old, white-headed man the colour of dry leather whose name was Dolores Rubio and since being *el mayór* paid nothing, his mayorship kept goats for milk and sheep for meat.

The residences in Mex town were uniquely alike; flat roofs, mud walls three feet thick and wherever there was shade, an overhang called a *texas*. The focal point was the old adobe mission church. So old, massively squatty and dusty no one's grandfather could recall it ever not having been there.

At one time, when *Mejico* still owned the South-west there had been a constabulary so there had been a barracks for *activos*, regular Mexican Army soldiers. But after the *Yanqui* conquest those Mexicans had departed and now the *commandante*'s post was the jailhouse and lawman's office.

His name was Carter Alvarado, half *gringo*, half Mex, a bad man to cross, at times overbearing, but the *gringos* who now controlled Angelina, the entire South-west for that matter, wanted law and order and under Carter Alvarado they got it.

Angelina was too distant from the border for vanquished revolutionaries to reach in their flight from *federales* which was a blessing. More southerly towns were consistently raided, but Angelina's seren-ity, summer languor and winter inertia were not inspiring for a different reason, the economy was weak and stagnant. There was little business, less trade and, except for the influx of predatory *gringos*, would have barely survived at subsistence level. Roast goat and *carnera*, mostly the latter because sheep are not to be milked and grow too much hair for coun-try where there is rarely enough shade, were the mainstay of local diets and had been for generations.

The freight trade brisked up during the spring and dwindled when full summer arrived. There was a *Yanqui* named Jim Elsworth who maintained a corral and mud barn in Angelina. He hauled freight both ways, from the southerly border country and from the northerly *Yanqui* country. He was a tough, weath-ered man in his late forties whose renown was based on the fact that although thieves, renegades, raiders of every kind, lived off stealing cattle, horses and mules for which there was always a market down in Mexico, he had never lost an animal. Twice he had been raided in the night, and twice he had tracked the thieves, shot them and returned with his animals, tucked up but otherwise uninjured.

Jim Elsworth brought freight to Hellsville. He and the black Irishman were enough of a kind that they had formed an enduring friendship.

It had been late spring when that holy man had been set upon by unfriendly spirits, the same time of year when Jim Elsworth, the freighter, arrived in Hell's Canyon with freight for the Irishman's store. He unloaded on Malone's dock out back, cared for his tough and tireless little Mexican mules and was bedded down in his wagon when Hell's Canyon's – not first – but most recent epic event occurred.

Jim Elsworth's four-up of mules were gone! The canyon had roads and trails which had animal tracks. Because there was no smithy in the Hellsville area, most shoeing was done at local forges. What Jim Elsworth and Rufus Malone discovered where the corral gate sagged open, was a variety of sign seen rarely in Hell's Canyon where there were dozens of horses, shod and barefoot, but very few mules of the big Missouri variety or the smaller and tougher Mexican.

Even more scarce were shod mule tracks. Jim Elsworth's Mexican mules were his family. He not only kept them shod but was so solicitous of their welfare other teamsters shook their heads.

Mule hooves were naturally narrower than horse hooves. Rufus Malone got two of his saddle animals after which he and Elsworth went scouring for mule sign. Clearly, whoever had stolen Elsworth's four mules had done the raiding before the night was well spent. The tracks led northward almost to the huge stone *barranca* which formed the northerly barrier of the canyon, and that used up the morning before the tracks veered westerly along the vertical stone bulwark and followed a cattle trail in that direction until the sun was slanting away. From that point, there was a thin notch in the *barranca* only used by hunters for an excellent reason. Following the trail, which was steep in places and not well defined, led up about where the topout was broodingly shadowed by virgin forest.

On the climb, they had paused often to 'blow' their mounts. It was at the last rest stop, with Elsworth looking up, that he asked if the storekeeper knew of Indians being up yonder.

Rufus, astride a 1200 pound bay gelding known locally for its 'bottom' said he'd hunted the uplands every autumn since coming into the canyon and had never seen an Indian or anything that made him suspect there were Indians up there.

Jim Elsworth plodded to the topout before dismounting and saying, 'Of my four mules only one was broke to ride. We been tracking mules and there hasn't been no sign of human feet even at the rest stops.'

Rufus Malone scowled. 'Which mule was broke to ride?'

'The one I called Estralita. Gentle as a lamb. Can be rode or drove. I've freighted nine years an' in all that time I never owned as all-around fine animal as my Estralita.'

Elsworth led his horse and took the lead. It was tricky business tracking in territory where a hundred generations of pine and fir trees had shed their needles. It was possible in this instance because the mules were shod.

They were about a mile deep sashaying in and out among huge trees when they came to a busy little cold water creek where Jim stopped, gestured for Rufus to climb down and pointed to the soft earth at creek-side.

When Rufus dismounted, his companion said, 'That there is a boot track, Rufe, not a moccasin track.' He was turning to mount when he also said, 'I'm goin' to hang that mule-stealing, son of a bitch so high the Almighty won't have to reach far to get his soul.'

Rufus followed his companion. The next time they halted he said, 'Jim, how did he know out of your four mules only one could be rode?'

Elsworth was slicing a corner off his chewing plug when he answered. 'He had to know which one could be rode.' After tucking the cud away, Jim Elsworth looked steadily at the storekeeper. 'Someone in your settlement?'

Malone had no answer. He knew every person in Hell's Canyon. If one was a horse- or mule-thief he couldn't imagine which one and he tried to fit the charge to a name as he followed his friend the *mulero*.

It was difficult to guess the time, stiff-topped old forest giants had been barring sunlight for a hundred years and more. Jim Elsworth didn't own a watch, had no use for one, and while Rufus Malone did own a watch, it was hanging on a peg back at the store. But he knew when he was hungry.

Jim Elsworth was one of those stringy, lanky men who had 'bottom'. He continued to follow the tracks until he came face to face with a huge boulder. There the sign veered around north-easterly and Jim halted, dismounted, scrambled up the huge boulder to see what was ahead, and the gunshot came out of nowhere, shattered rock near Jim's feet and he dropped the full distance to the ground.

Rufe had his six-gun in hand when he handed Jim his reins and started stalking around the far side of the massive rock.

Jim said, 'No. Rufe, come back!'

Malone looked over his shoulder. 'Take the other side,' he said, and Elsworth answered harshly, 'He knows where we are. Maybe there's more'n one.'

Rufe turned back disgusted and angry. 'You want your mules back? Then let's go get 'em.' Elsworth scoured for a rock, found one and hurled it toward the east side of their big boulder. Nothing happened, nor did Rufus expect it to. In his opinion that had been a schoolboy trick.

Malone's irritability vanished when the invisible gunman said, 'Go back!'

The mule-hunters exchanged a startled look. It had been a woman's voice. The accent was unmistakable. A female Mexican woman!

Jim Elsworth spoke. 'I don't go nowhere without my mules!'

This time the person they could not see said, '*Por favor*, go back.'

Rufus Malone moved soundlessly toward the easterly curve of the huge rock and motioned for the mule-man to go around the opposite side.

Rufus got belly-down, pushed his six-gun out and

cocked it. The woman said, '*No, señors.* Go back.'

From the other side of the rock, Elsworth sounded exasperated when he spoke. 'I told you, not without my mules. What are you, a female horse-thief?'

This time there was no response. Over where Rufus Malone was creeping forward, he saw a shadowy movement and tipped up his six-gun. The shadow moved clear of a huge old fir tree and stood with a Winchester cradled in one arm. She was looking in the opposite direction.

Rufus eased down the dog of his weapon, leathered it and carefully got to his feet. The distance was not great, but when she saw him all she had to do was twist and fire.

Jim Elsworth called again. 'What the hell is a woman goin' to do with four mules?'

The answer he got sounded unsteady to Rufus. 'It was what I had to do. The store was locked.'

Rufus started walking. When the woman turned, saw him coming, she faced him bringing up the carbine. She said, '*Por favor*, I don't want to shoot you.'

On the far side of the rock, Jim Elsworth stepped into view with his cocked six-gun aimed.

Rufus got close, took the saddle gun in both hands because he expected resistance. The woman did not resist. She seemed relieved not to have the carbine. As they looked at one another the woman bit her lip hard, but tears came anyway.

Elsworth came up, stood relaxed and gently wagging his head. 'Where are my mules?'

The woman turned without speaking. They followed her, wary of whoever she was with. They came to a small clearing where a lowering sun showed four mules cropping grass. The woman led halfway around on the east side of the clearing, stopped, turned and said, 'Please . . . he is too sick to hold a gun. Please. . . .'

The camp was nondescript and untidy, what there was of it. The man, lying motionless, watching the strangers following his woman, didn't have the strength to do more than make a feeble, fluttery gesture toward a nearby shellbelted holster.

Rufus let go a loud sigh. Jim turned to look out where his mules were contentedly grazing, then looked back as the woman emptied the holster the man on old blankets had tried to reach.

The woman knelt to take one limp hand between her two hands. Jim Elsworth moved closer as a slowly gathering frown ridged his forehead. He said, 'Wayne?'

The prone man answered softly, 'Mister Elsworth.'

Rufus knelt beside the ailing individual looking for some indication of what had put him down. The woman opened the shirt and Malone caught his breath. The infection was dripping. Rufe leaned to probe and look closer after which he leaned back to ask a guestion.

'Gunshot?'

The woman answered. 'Five days ago. We tried to rob a store. The lawman was buying a sack of tobacco. He shot my man. We stole two horses and rode north. Three nights ago, a cougar scared the horses. I looked for them but they were gone.'

Jim Elsworth rocked back on his heels. 'The last time I saw you, was with Old Man Haggard's drive to rails' head. What happened?'

Rufus was examining the hot swelling with two

fingers. He bruised the hottest point and pus poured over his hand.

2

A Burying

Malone went to wash his hands beside a piddling creek. As he was arising, the mule-man came up, blew out a ragged breath and, while looking where his mules were eating, said, 'It was the store down at Angelina.'

'You know him?'

'Wayne Holser. Years back, before I went to freighting, him an' me went to partnering on trail drives. It's been a while.' Elsworth turned. 'It's been six, seven years. We met down at Eagle Pass. . . . Rufe, that bullet hit him in the back. The woman got him this far. They didn't get no money at the store. She saw my mules from the topout. She saw your store, too, but was afraid to try another robbery, so she drove my mules back up here. She told me she figured to sell them.'

'Where? Everyone knows your mules, Jim.'

Elsworth turned back to watch his mules. 'She didn't know where. Rufe, she's worried sick and scairt.' Eleworth paused again. 'He'll die, Rufe. He's hot to the touch. Gawd damn! He never done anythin' to deserve this.'

Malone searched for words and came up with

16

some that even sounded ridiculous to him. 'I can go down to Angelina an' bring back the doctor.'

'Too late, Rufe. You saw him. I'm goin' out to see the mules.'

Rufus Malone watched his old friend walk through tall grass and returned to the camp where the woman looked from a set of features held rigid to hide emotion.

Rufe knelt beside the wounded man, said his name and, for the life of him, couldn't think of anything else to say until the flushed-faced man spoke. 'He's a good man, Mister. . . .'

'Rufe.'

'Rufe. We hoorawed a lot of towns on the trail to Kansas. Those were days I never forgot.'

'Wayne, was it the law down yonder that shot you?'

'Yes. I made a mistake. I never done a hold-up before. I should've walked in first. If I'd seen the lawman I'd've just walked out. Rufe, we been livin' hard, berries where we find 'em, brush rabbits. I had fifteen dollars. I lost it in a poker game. Rufe, that slug went plumb through me. 'Cept for Maria Elena . . . we come a hell of a distance. She saw 'em fannin' out from that town, she got us this far, since then she's been watchin'. Rufe, I don't know you. I'm dyin', friend. Maybe tonight. When Jim comes back tell him if he'll look after her I'll put in a good word for him – somewhere. You wouldn't have a tad of whiskey, would you?'

Rufe shook his head, there was whiskey at the store, but before he could go back there and return. . . . He said, 'Wayne, for Chris' sake. . . .'

'I know. But we was plumb out of money.'

Rufe heard Jim coming, arose and took him aside.

When Elsworth spoke he said, 'Tonight? I've seen hurt folks before but. . . .'

'He said if you'd take care of the woman he'd put in a good word for you where he's goin'.'

'There's no justice in this gawddamned world, Rufe. He's as good a man as you'd ever ride a trail with.'

The woman came soundlessly which was unusual because she was wearing boots. She looked from Rufe to Jim, without speaking, so Elsworth said, 'Him an' I was partners, years back. Wayne's a good man.'

She held back tears, but the strain showed in her face. 'I left a bad man to go with him.' Her gaze swung to Elsworth. 'We would get married. . . .'

Rufe abruptly left the woman and Jim went over to sit beside his friend and speak softly. 'Wayne, why'n hell didn't you hunt up a doctor?' Instead of an answer he got a weak sardonic smile. 'No time. Jim, I need a favour.'

'Shoot.'

'Look out for her. She's as sweet an' carin' a female as you'll ever meet. Will you. . . ?'

Elsworth nodded. 'Rest easy. For as long as she wants. Does she have kin?'

'An older sister is all.'

'Where?'

'A place called Bogus down near Laredo. You'd maybe remember. Bogus is about five miles east of Coltville. But she won't go back. The miserable son of a bitch she was married to lives in Bogus. He beat hell out of her. She's got scars, an' he hit her in the gut so hard she lost their baby. Jim?'

'Don't worry, partner.'

In forested high country there was no dusk. One

half-hour there was sooty light, the next half-hour it was night. Maria Elena made a meal of rabbit mixed with the last of the cornmeal. No one ate. When she took a tin bowl over to her man he was asleep. She put the bowl aside, put both hands on his chest and prayed.

Rufe and the *mulero* walked out to visit with the mules and Jim said, 'I'd have given him the mules. Excuse me.'

Rufe watched his friend walk out among the animals keeping his back turned.

Rufe spent almost an hour hobbling the saddle animals. There were only two of them, hobbling gentle horses usually required about fifteen minutes.

He could see Jim Elsworth leaning across one mule's back, head down. He went back to the camp.

Rarely were rangemen good with sidearms. Lawmen were.

When he returned to the camp, the woman was kneeling with her man's hand in her lap.

When the moon came, it shone in the little clearing but nowhere else. Rufe stood still. It was probably his imagination but moonlight seemed brighter in the meadow.

He made his way back and the woman looked up from her kneeling position, unabashedly crying. Rufe brushed her shoulder with the tips of his fingers. She jack-knifed up to her feet and fell against him. Rufus Malone knew very little about women. This night he didn't have to as he raised both powerful arms and held her until the front of his shirt was soaked.

He would have traded a spanking new saddle for a jolt of whiskey. Somewhere among the big fir trees, across the clearing easterly, an owl sounded. Usually they got answers. This one didn't nor did it call again.

Jim came up, rolled and lighted a smoke and softly addressed the woman. 'When you skirted around the big canyon you could have come down there.'

She shook her head without speaking, pulled clear of Rufe and walked where the trees were thickest. After she was gone, Rufe said, 'How old was he?'

Jim didn't know, nor did it matter. 'About my age. Maybe twenty-nine or thirty. We did our share of hell-raisin'. Over the years I wondered what become of him.'

'He's got kin somewhere?'

'Orphan, Rufe. You know, he never said much about them things.'

They went over to the ragged, soiled old bedroll. Wayne neither opened his eyes nor moved but he was shallowly breathing.

'Jim?'

'Yes.'

'We got no digging tools.'

Elsworth nodded slowly. 'I wouldn't want to bury him up here. Wolves, bears'n coyotes'd dig him up.' He looked squarely at the storekeeper. 'Could we take him back down yonder?'

Rufe nodded. There would be curiosity. In Hellsville there was little of interest. Rufe and the freighter bringing back a dead man to be buried would start talk.

Maria Elena didn't sleep that night. She was kneeling, holding a hand in her lap while both men slept, as much from emotional draining as from manhunting exhaustion.

Jim awakened first as dawn was breaking. He would probably have slept longer but for a jay bird in an overhead tangle of branches which did as most animals do after a long night's sleep. He relieved himself.

Jim sat up, reached for a nearby saddle blanket and wiped his shirt. Ordinarily he would have routed the bird with profanity and whatever came to hand that could be thrown. The reason he did not act as other men would have was because in the dust-free, golden, first sun rays he saw Maria Elena lying beside his old partner, one arm across Wayne's chest, one of his arms across her shoulders. She was asleep; Wayne was dead.

He went to the puny creek to wash. Rufe joined him. He hadn't awakened the woman when he leaned to feel cold flesh. As he was washing he said, 'Passed on last night, Jim.'

Elsworth nodded, he didn't need to have been told. As he was drying his face with a faded bandanna he stood up and said, 'I figured last night or today. Rufe, you mind if we pack him down yonder?'

'Mind? Of course not.'

'The woman can ride Estralita, the others'll follow her.'

They rigged out the horses. Jim made a squaw bridle out of a length of rope and fitted it to Estralita who seemed not to mind.

While Maria Elena was washing at the creek, they got Wayne across one of the mules. Considering they had no pack outfit and only a pair of lariats which they had to cut, they did a good job. It was Jim's idea to take the best blanket from the dead man's bedroll and cover him with it before they finished the lashings.

Jim got the woman astraddle Estralita. She helped

as much as she could with an expressionless face, puffy from lack of sleep and tears. She neither spoke nor looked at the men.

On the trail back, as long as they threaded their way through timber it was cool and shadowy. Sunshine did not reach them until they paused atop the *barranca* overlooking Hell's Canyon.

The downward trail was both crooked and narrow, in the places where horses might have had trouble the mules didn't.

It required more time going back than it had required going up. For one thing they did not have to 'favour'. It was either level or sloping southward. Another factor was time; they had spent quite a bit of it preparing for the departure and during the ride where huge trees created obstacles they had to sashay a lot.

When they finally left the cliff and started downward, the day was well along. The heat helped; it kept people indoors or at least in tree shade.

They left the trail where the canyon floor met them and Rufe didn't take the most direct route to his store, he used pathways and, although being unseen was not possible, they made it around back to the store's loading dock without interference. They put Wayne Holser in the cooler shed out behind the store. Its walls were adobe, three feet thick. No one knew who had originally built it but because it followed the traditional south country pattern, its builder had to have been a Mexican.

Rufe took his companions inside through the loading dock door and did not unlock the front door which didn't matter, there was no one waiting. It was getting close to supper-time.

He got some bottles of peaches, salt beef and set them on the counter. He didn't expect the woman to eat, but after knowing the freighter as long as he had he expected Elsworth to fish forth his clasp knife and eat.

He didn't. But he spoke. 'We can bury him tonight, Rufe.'

Maria Elena turned her back.

Malone nodded but without enthusiasm. It had been a long, difficult two days, but weariness would have to wait. He took Maria Elena to his cubbyhole office, pointed to an old iron cot, asked if she would like something to eat and, when she declined, he returned to the counter, told Jim Elsworth to get some rest, that after nightfall they would do the burying. The later the better.

When he was alone, Rufe pulled a pair of army blankets from a shelf and bedded on the floor behind his counter out of sight.

He slept until someone kicked the bottom of his boots. Elsworth looked like hell; beard stubble was part of it; his face was drawn; his eyes lacked normal lustre. As Rufe stood up, the freighter said, 'I found two shovels out back. Rufe, what about her?'

Rufe went quietly to peek into the cubbyhole office. Maria Elena was breathing evenly in long breaths. She would sleep a long time.

The Hellsville cemetery was in a part of useless land where scrub brush and oak trees grew. It had about ten or eleven headboards and two elaborate graves marked by stone reminders.

It was chilly. Since time out of mind it had turned chilly any time of year after the sun sank behind the high westerly rims.

The first foot of digging required crowbars more than shovels, after that the earth had enough moisture so that crowbars were not needed.

They rested often, looked and listened. The nearest habitation was a good 400 yards and belonged to an ancient hide-hunter and his equally as ancient wife, neither of whom could hear any noise less than someone striking an anvil.

They squared the four sides. The last half distance they had to get down into the hole. When Jim used his shovel handle to measure depth he leaned the implement aside, brought forth a pony of whiskey from a hip pocket and held it out.

Rufe drank, handed it back, put his shovel aside and said, 'It's deep enough. You ready?'

A dog barked before they reached the cooler shed. As they were carrying their load back the dog barked again. This time it scouted for scent, found the men and furiously barked until Jim routed it with small rocks.

Rufe was uncomfortable. After they lowered Wayne inside his army blanket and stood with their shovels looking down, he said, 'You know any prayers, Jim?'

'One. Learnt it when I was small.'

'You want to say it?'

Elsworth went through the entire Lord's Prayer from memory, then went to work filling in where they had recently excavated.

After mounding the grave to allow for settling, Jim said he would someday have a headboard made and they had another pull on the bottle and started back. They were sweat soaked and bone tired. Neither of them said a word, but when they entered the store from out back, Jim said he had to go care for his mules and Rufe tiptoed through to the front of the store and got a shock.

Maria Elena was standing in front of the counter. In weak light she looked very young. In fact, she was twenty. She had also combed her hair and had washed somewhere.

Rufe self-consciously leaned the shovels aside. When he turned she said, 'You should have wakened me.'

They probably should have. Neither of them had thought of it.

'Will you show me the grave when it is light?'

'Yes. Jim mentioned someday he'd have a marker made. There's a feller down in Angelina who can carve better'n anyone I ever saw.'

She nodded without speaking for a while. 'Where is Wayne's friend?'

'Bedded down. He's a freighter. That's his rig beyond the cooler house.' Rufus went to a bench and sat down. His back was painful. It only noticeably bothered him when he did manual labour, like digging a grave.

Maria Elena said, 'If I could borrow two dollars from you I would leave. Is there a way to get out where there is a stage?'

Before he answered, Rufus leaned far back, remained that way for a long moment then sat forward. 'There's no regular way to get to Angelina from here, but almost every day someone goes down there for supplies.' He paused, looking steadily at her. 'When you went to rob the store in Angelina, did you go inside with Wayne?'

'I was out front holding the horses.'

Rufus arose, went to the front window and stood there looking out. Distantly, breakfast-fire smoke was rising; closer, people were appearing. He turned. 'Maria Elena, if they saw him they saw you. I don't think it'd be a good idea for you to go back there. Not for a spell anyway.'

She didn't move from her leaning position against the counter. 'What can I do? I can't stay here.'

'Why not? Looks to me to be the onliest safe place for you, for a spell anyway.'

She crossed to the bench he had vacated, sat with both hands in her lap staring at the floor. 'If I had two dollars I could start walking.' She stood up. 'I left a small bundle on the bed. Someday I will come back for it.'

He wished Jim were beside him, although Elsworth didn't know her any better than Rufe did.

He braced before speaking. 'Listen to me. You can have two dollars. You can have ten dollars. . . . Maria Elena, where can you. . . ? They are hunting you an' . . . Wayne. If they wasn't, a woman walking alone . . . beyond this canyon it's a big country. Even if they didn't recognize you, aside from Angelina there aren't any settlements for fifty miles. No! You can't do that. If Jim was here he'd tell you. For a while even here in the canyon. . . . You can't hide.'

She continued to look up at him. 'I will walk to that town and tell them who I am.'

Rufus glanced around the store. Dawn light was brightening the world; it was brightening the inside of the store. 'You can stay where you slept last night. I'll bring some food and water.' Rufe was feeling desperate. Not entirely for her. If they caught her, and they surely would, and she mentioned Wayne or the two men who had helped her. . . .

He said, 'Come with me.'

Dutifully she followed him to the little cluttered office. There was a chair with one short leg, the cot and the table he used for the store. He would have preferred something better for her, but at the moment he couldn't think of anything.

She stood looking at him and spoke as though she had read his mind. 'They won't be looking for you.'

He didn't argue, he simply said, 'Make yourself as comfortable as you can. I know it's not much. I'll fetch something to eat and a jug of water. Maria Elena. . . ? Please don't leave this room. I'll find Jim. Between us we'll figure something . . . you promise?'

'I won't leave the room. Tonight you could take me to the grave?'

'Yes'm. Now wait an hour or so. The eatery will be open, I'll get you something to eat.'

He left and Maria Elena sank down on the cot, which was old with a lumpy, corn-husk mattress but it was better than the ground.

She heard him unlock the front door, heard people talking and worried because the cubbyhole had no door. It was, however, at the back of the store well away from the area customers would have reason to go.

3

She Stays!

When Jim appeared he had scrubbed, shaved and changed his shirt and britches. He looked so presentable Rufe said, 'All you need is grease on your boots.'

Jim asked about Maria Elena. Rufe sent him to the little store office and moments later he got his first sensation of stomach trouble.

Three men tied up out front at the hitch rack. He knew all three of them. One was Carter Alvarado, the other two were the big rawboned storekeeper from Angelina, Arthur Kemp, and the third man from Angelina was Homer Helm called Jake, Angelina's town blacksmith.

When they entered the store none of them was smiling and Marshal Alvarado said, 'We been trackin', Rufe. A feller tried to rob Art's store some days back. He had a Mex woman with him. She held their horses, two bays, an' when they made a run for it I shot the feller.' Having said all this, Marshal Alvarado leaned on the counter before saying more. 'Tracks led here, in the canyon. Because I don't expect you get many strangers ridin' sweaty horses we figured you or others saw 'em. Maybe the woman at the eatery, I'll get to her directly. Right now, anyone come to your store for medicine or bandagin'; or maybe food?'

Rufe could answer that with a clear conscience. 'No strangers been here that I've seen an' I don't stock bandagin' cloth. You shot him, Carter?'

'As they was racin' out the north end of town. The damned fool; I was buyin' a sack of tobacco in the store when he came in wavin' his six-gun. I think he was hard hit. The last I saw he was ridin' hunched over. Rufe, he couldn't have gone far. Maybe someone's hidin' him in the canyon.'

Rufe shook his head. 'Not unless he had kin here. Hell's Canyon folks just don't cotton to any kind of strangers, shot ones or un-shot ones.'

Marshal Alvarado straightened up almost smiling. 'Obliged, Rufe. We'll circulate an' ask around.'

Rufe thought that was a good idea and said so. After the men from Angelina left, he went to the cubbyhole office where Jim Elsworth and Maria Elena were sitting like owls.

Jim spoke first. 'Now what do we do? How long'll they stay?'

Before Rufe could reply, Maria Elena repeated what she had told Rufe before, 'I'll leave. I'll watch so no one finds me.'

Jim said almost the exact words Rufe had used to this suggestion. 'How an' where'll you go? Someone'll sure as hell see you. By now, for miles around, folks know what happened in Angelina.' He sounded as exasperated as he felt. 'You can hide here. If no one sees you. . . .'

Someone called from out front. 'Rufus! Rufus Malone where'n hell are you!'

Jim looked up. 'Beulah.'

Rufe left the office. The woman he met at the counter was squinty-eyed, dowdy, sixtyish and clearly annoyed. Her name was Beulah Bell. She operated the eatery and, oddly enough, despite her looks and disposition was a good cook.

She glared. 'How do you expect to run a store never bein' where folks can find you!'

Rufe went behind the counter. 'What can I do for you?' he asked and got a shock.

The dowdy woman said, 'What was you'n that stringbean of a freighter doin' out in the graveyard last night? An' don't tell me it wasn't you. I went out to pee, heard shovellin' an' walked a ways until I saw you both, and this mornin' when I walked out there in broad daylight there was a fresh grave.'

Rufe rubbed his jaw. 'It was dark last night; it could have been anyone out there, Beulah.'

'It wasn't anybody, it was you'n that freighter. I saw you both. Rufe, two o'clock in the mornin' is a hell of a time to be buryin' folks unless someone got murdered an' you'n that freighter done it an' buried him.'

Jim Elsworth appeared from the gloomy rear of the store. He and Maria Elena had heard every word as clearly as they'd heard the men from Angelina. Jim's expression was set in stone. He stopped a few feet from the woman and said, 'Like hell you went out to pee. You've had a habit of prowlin' in the night for whatever you can steal. Beulah, you tell that story an' so help me I'll burn you out!'

The dowdy woman was not intimidated. She had the disposition of a bear with a sore behind and faced Elsworth, squinting harder than usual when she said, 'I forgot your name, but mister, I saw you'n him out there diggin' a grave. Mister, that was stupid. Every other grave out there's had grass growing on 'em for years. You think folks won't notice? That pain in the butt of a lawman from Angelina come by my eatery askin' questions. If they go meanderin' they're goin' to find that fresh grave.'

Before Jim could speak Rufe said, 'What did you tell 'em?'

'Tell who? Oh, that loggerhead of a town marshal? I told 'em far as I knew there hadn't been no strangers in the canyon since that trapper come through last spring. An' that's the gospel truth.'

'What else did they ask you?' Rufe wanted to know.

'He said it was a man an' a Mex woman an' that he shot the man, an' that they tracked 'em to the front of the canyon.' Beulah paused looking steadily at Jim Elsworth. 'So that's it. You buried the outlaw Marshal Pisshead is lookin' for.' She looked from Jim to Rufe. 'Why would you two bury a dead outlaw?'

When neither man answered, the dowdy woman brushed back loose grey hair, went to a bench, sat down and said, 'What'd you do with the Messican woman? Knowin' you two I'd say she's in mighty poor hands. You figure to keep her for a pet? Well, cat's got your tongues, has it?'

Rufe and Jim exchanged a look which the woman saw and acidly commented on. 'That lawman an' his friends're bound to turn up somethin' even if they don't find that fresh grave.'

'How?' Jim surlily asked. 'You're goin' to tell him?'

Beulah snorted, 'Me, help the law? Sonny whatever-your-name is, before he died nine years ago I was married to the best train robber who ever come down the draw. Me help that back-shootin' son of a bitch? Not as long as I can draw a breath. Where's the Mex woman?'

From the gloom a quiet voice, 'Here.'

Beulah stared. Maria Elena looked younger than her twenty years in the shadows. After a long period of silence, Beulah spoke again. 'Is that your man these two whelps buried out yonder last night?'

Maria Elena came closer. 'His name was Wayne Holser. We were going to get married.'

Beulah snorted again. 'They all say that. How old are you?'

'Twenty. He was a good man.'

Beulah spoke again. 'Maybe, but what kind of a damned fool walks into a store in broad daylight wavin' a gun where a lawman is standin'? What's your name?'

'Maria Elena. What's your name?'

'Beulah Bell. I own the eatery. Maria Elena. That's a pretty name. You better come home with me. Stay away from these two. I know their kind.'

Beulah stood up looking at Rufe. 'Is the loading dock door locked?' When Rufe shook his head Beulah faced Maria Elena. 'Come along,' she said and led the way. Neither Rufe nor Jim made an attempt to stop them, and after the back door had been slammed Jim went to the bench, sat down and looked at the storekeeper. Rufe scratched his unruly mane and sighed. 'That Beulah took her don't bother me as much as who else went out to pee last night.'

Jim wasn't ready to abandon the subject of the two women. He said, 'If there's a bounty, Beulah might be willin' to sell her to the law, an' if she does that, we'll be in trouble up to our gullets.'

Rufe leaned on the counter. 'For what, buryin' a man we found up yonder?'

'For helpin' his woman to hide, to start with, an' for buryin' Wayne knowin' he got shot tryin' to rob the store down in Angelina, an' I'd guess Marshal Alvarado'll figure out other charges.'

A woman carrying a net shopping bag came in out of the sunlight. It was always cool in the store which had no windows and just two doors.

While Rufe waited on the woman, Jim left by the back door to go see how his hobbled mules were faring out a ways from the settlement. Later, he headed back, but veered off to visit the eatery. Beulah was removing dishes where a recent diner had been and put her unfriendly gaze on the teamster as she said, 'I forgot your name.'

As Jim eased down at the counter and swatted at a large blue-tailed fly, he said his name first, then spelled it and looked up to be met by a bleak squinty stare. 'What was you figurin' to do with Maria Elena? Don't lie to me; there's two things I know, cookin' an' men.'

Jim nodded toward the coffee urn. She got him a cup, set it in front of him and spoke again. 'That peehead lawman is still pokin' around askin' questions.' She leaned down. 'You'n Rufe an' Marshal Alvarado make a team. You'n Rufe couldn't pour pee out of an open-toed boot an' the lawman isn't no smarter; nevertheless, he's bound to come up with somethin'. His kind can fall down in a gut yard an' come up smellin' of roses. Given enough time. . . .'

'Are you goin' to feed me or preach a damned sermon?'

Beulah disappeared behind an army blanket, the divider between her cooking area and the counter. From back there she called to Elsworth, 'Maria Elena told me the whole story. She should've shot her husband. I would have.'

Jim called back sourly, 'I could skin a horse in less time than you can rassle me somethin' to eat.'

That ended their exchange. An hour later with the sun teetering atop the westerly, high-forested rims, Rufe went looking for Jim Elsworth. Marshal Alvarado and his pair of stone-faced possemen had returned with a scrap of information that Rufe listened to with misgivings. Alvarado had found one of the horses folks in Angelina had described to him as being ridden by the man he shot and his woman. It had been found with saddle galls by a pot hunter about three miles west of the canyon. The pot hunter had brought it back with him. He showed the corralled animal to the marshal. The pot hunter had washed its back and salved the galls. He also gave the lawman directions to the area where he had found the horse.

Jim was at his wagon and listened to what Rufus had to relate and for the first time in several days Elsworth smiled. 'He'll go back where the horse was found an' that's good. Get him out of the canyon.'

'There was blood on the saddle,' Rufe said, and Jim continued to smile.

'He'll be way to hell an' gone westerly lookin' for his wounded outlaw.' Jim paused. 'I know how to get Maria Elena away. See that place under the seat where I keep tools an' tinned food? She'll just about fit in there.'

Rufe craned to look at the place beneath the

wagon seat and nodded. It wouldn't be comfortable, but for as long as she'd be in there wouldn't be as long as she'd spend in prison.

He leaned back. 'When?'

'I got to reset Estralita's shoes in the mornin'. We can leave in the afternoon.'

Rufe returned to the store where an irate customer had been waiting. It was one of the outlying stockmen. He said when a body ran a store he'd ought to be handy when customers came by. Rufe agreed and went about piling the cowman's requirements on the counter. As the rancher was paying he said, 'What's the matter with Beulah? When I went in to get fed she was crankier'n usual.'

Rufe helped the stockman carry his supplies to a battered old ranch wagon, returned to the store his earlier euphoria over the prospect of getting rid of Maria Elena bothered by an unpleasant thought. If Beulah saw Elsworth expected to spirit Maria Elena out of the canyon she'd raise hell and that is exactly what she did although Beulah did not go look at the wagon. Elsworth told her and she went looking for Rufe.

When they met she pulled herself up to her full height, gave Rufe a squinty-eyed, hostile look and said, 'You can't make that girl leave here. She don't have a friend in the world an' she's not only scairt she's most likely someone's daughter.'

Rufe looked at the older woman. He hadn't expected this reason for disagreement. 'Beulah, she's got a sister in Texas an' that's all the family she's got.'

'Texas? It might as well be the moon. An' how's she goin' to get to Texas, her with no money, pretty as a picture an' alone? I fixed up my extra bedroom for her. You told her you'd bring her somethin' to eat an' you never did. She ate like a horse. She stays here!'

Rufe went back to Jim's wagon and told him what Beulah had said. Jim reddened. 'That danged old harpy. Wayne's woman's got to be got plumb away from here. The further the better. Rufe, suppose the law catches her, she'll say how we buried Wayne an' hid her from Marshal Alvarado.'

Rufe considered his friend. 'You think she'd ought to stay? Why'n hell did you come up with that idea of sneakin' her away in your wagon?'

'I figured to give her a little money in exchange for her promise not to say you'n me helped her an' buried Wayne.'

Rufe showed his disgust, but he didn't argue; he said, 'All right, she stays,' and returned to the store not just disgusted but worried.

He forgot he had said he would take her to her man's grave.

He was locking up for the night when she knocked on the rear door and when he admitted her she said he wouldn't have to show her the grave she and Beulah had found it.

Rufe stood in the doorway staring. 'You'n Beulah went out there in broad daylight?'

She nodded. 'Someone else had been there. Beulah said the boot tracks we saw belonged to three men, not just the two tracks you and the freighter might have made.'

After she left once again, Rufe went hunting for the freight wagon. Jim was working on Estralita's feet and looked up annoyedly until Rufe repeated what he had been told, then Jim put the foot down. 'Three sets of tracks? Would that be Alvarado and his friends?'

Jim's answer was curt. 'You know any other three men who'd be out there?'

Jim clutched his hoof nippers in one hand. 'We got to get her away from here. Far away, an' she's got to promise not to tell anyone about us.'

Rufe shook his head. 'She's the only one can get us trouble. She stays, Jim.'

Rufe returned to the store, made sure the place was locked tight and went to Beulah's place for something to eat and got a shock. It wasn't Beulah who came to wait on him, it was Maria Elena!

Rufe got up, stormed around the counter into the cooking area where Beulah looked up from her work. He said, 'What in the hell's wrong with you?'

Before he could say more, the squinty-eyed older woman said, 'She wants to be helpful, an' she needs somethin' to keep her from thinkin'.'

'Beulah, you know they got her description.'

'They're gone. I saw 'em leavin' by the westerly trail.'

'Hell, Beulah, they talked to folks around here, an' you come up with a woman folks haven't seen before.'

The dowdy, older woman put her fry pan away from the fire and faced Rufe with both hands on her hips. 'I got a story worked up. She come along lookin' for work an' I hired . . .'

'Beulah, Chris' A'mighty. They know a Mex woman was with the feller they're huntin'. How many pretty Mex females even know where the canyon is let alone come wanderin' in? Beulah. *They got her description!*'

She interrupted him again. 'Rufus, she's got no kin, no money. She's about as close to havin' a broken spirit as a person can get. Now, if you want to eat get out of my kitchen an' go set at the counter!'

Rufe briefly lingered, protest and profanity dammed up behind his teeth in about equal parts, then stamped back to the counter and sat down.

Maria Elena had to have heard every word from the kitchen, but she smiled at him as she said, 'Antelope steak, garlic potatoes, coffee and pie.'

He scowled. 'Garlic potatoes?'

'I made them. I grew up eating them. My mother said potatoes have no taste unless it's cooked into them.'

'What kind of pie?'

'Blueberry. Beulah made it.'

'No garlic?'

Her smile lingered. 'No garlic. Do you want your coffee black?'

He was tempted to say black was the only way folks drank coffee. Instead he bobbed his head up and down and, after Maria Elena departed, Rufe twisted to look into the roadway. It was empty. It usually was. Folks in the canyon patronized the eatery when they were caught too far from home.

Jim Elsworth came in beating dust off with his hat. He saw Rufe alone at the counter and hesitated before approaching. As he was easing down, Rufe told him who Beulah's waitress was and the freighter reacted philosophically. 'Like you said, she stays,' and when the handsome girl appeared Jim ordered as though he hadn't expected anyone else to appear for his order.

She smiled at him, asked how he liked his coffee

and disappeared into the kitchen.

Rufe was disconsolately solemn until after their meals arrived then he turned, knife and fork poised and said, 'You know what, Jim?'

'No, I don't know what. What?'

'We're stuck with her an' sure as I'm settin' here we're goin' to wish we'd left her up yonder with your friend.'

Elsworth had a mouthful, had to wash it down before he could reply, but he eventually said, 'To tell you the gospel truth, while I was cleanin' out the box under my wagon seat I was tryin' hard to figure some way I wouldn't have to sneak her out of the canyon.'

Rufe ate in dogged silence. His friend's revelation didn't surprise him but its implication drove him deeper into his dark mood. Jim Elsworth and Maria Elena?

Maria Elena would stay!

4

Getting in Deeper

It rained, which was not unusual although most storms passed over Hell's Canyon.

People whose livelihood depended upon animals welcomed rain, their opposites who dwelt in towns did not welcome it. For one thing, it made roads treacherously slippery. For another thing, merchants suffered because shoppers as a rule stayed close to stoves and fireplaces.

Rufus Malone only had three customers for the two days the rain fell, both were woman shoppers whose requirements were minimal.

It was two days after the rain clouds had passed westerly and the ground had ceased steaming under sunlight that his sense of security which had been increasing, was shattered.

Town Marshal Carter Alvarado and his pair of dogged townsmen appeared in the store and, as before, they were both cryptic and unsmiling.

Alvarado put some soggy, soiled cloth on the countertop which Rufe recognized even as he said, 'You gents get caught out in the rain?'

Alvarado ignored the question, leaned down look-

40

ing steadily at Rufus as he said, 'We backtracked, found the other horse with the saddle under its belly an' full of gas from eating with the bit in its mouth. It was close to where the pot hunter found the other one.'

Rufe interrupted. 'Bad shape was it?'

For the second time the marshal ignored the question. 'We backtracked up into the timber. The tracks was clear. We come onto the place where them bloody rags an' some other things showed where the feller I shot an' his woman had a camp. Looked to us like they spent some time there. My guess is that he was hit hard an' likely died up there. Someone else was up there an' there was mule sign. The body was gone so we followed mule sign. Someone packed the dead feller down here. Puttin' two an' two together. . . . There's a fresh grave out yonder. Folks we talked to said no one'd been buried out there for at least a year. Rufe, who's got mules except Jim Elsworth?'

Everything the lawman had said weakened Rufe's resolve. He answered in a quiet way. 'Elsworth's mules aren't the onliest ones in the canyon.'

Alvarado nodded. 'You're right. We spent most of yestiddy lookin' up stockmen for mules, an' we found some. But not a one was shod. Jim Elsworth keeps his mules shod.'

Jake Helm the blacksmith spoke up. 'Rufe, who's in the grave out yonder?'

A tall, rawboned old man walked in. His name was Josh Henley. He'd been a buffalo hunter until that business expired and since then had been a pot hunter who sold meat as far off as Angelina.

He considered the lawmen, walked up to the

counter and ignored them as he told Rufe he wanted
a plug of Mule Shoe, which Rufe got and put atop
the counter. The old hunter dug into a purse, put a
five-cent piece down and picked up the tobacco plug,
pocketed it and spoke at the same time.

'I didn't know Beulah's husband was an In'ian.'

Rufe didn't know that either. Marshal Alvarado
was on occasion an impatient man. He interrupted
to say, 'Rufe, if it's him in the grave, fine, but the
woman's still loose.'

The old hunter winked at Rufe and left the store
using the same shambling gait he'd used when he'd
entered.

Alvarado acted as though there had been no interruption. 'Where's Jim Elsworth?'

'With his mules, I expect,' Rufe replied.

Alvarado eyed the storekeeper steadily. 'There was
sign of two riders with the mules coming down out of
the uplands where we found that camp.'

Rufe shrugged and the marshal added a few more
words. 'Two horsemen, four shod mules an' one
sashayin' among trees like maybe it was packed.'

Alvarado straightened up. Told his companions it
was time to eat, nodded at Rufe and led the way out
of the store.

Rufe didn't move for a long few minutes. He'd
heard tales about Marshal Alvarado but he'd never
heard Alvarado was a good tracker and a *coyote*
lawman, but clearly he was both.

Rufe hiked past the eatery on his way to find Jim
and saw Beulah waiting on the trio from Angelina.

Jim was hand-soaping harness in the shade. Within
sight, his mules were picking at grass and browse.
Rufe wasted no time on niceties. He told the

freighter almost word for word what had been said at the store.

Jim dunked both hands in a collapsible water-proofed canvas bucket to rid his hands of Probert's soap, dried them down the outside seams of his trousers and said, 'We can still get her away. Only it seems to me we'd do better to hide her in Hellsville. Alvarado can't just go rummagin' in folks's stores an' houses lookin' for her. He'll get himself shot.'

Rufe eased down on the sloping wagon tongue. 'It's too late for that, Jim. Alvarado's smarter'n I figured. He figured who's in the damned grave. He figured the rest of it about like it happened. Jim, they went to Beulah's place to get fed. Alvarado'll be lookin' you up directly. Why'n hell do you keep them mules shod?'

Elsworth frowned. 'To protect their feet. Them mules is all I got. They're my family. . . . He read the sign?'

Rufe nodded. 'Like a 'coon dog. Him or Jake Helm or . . .'

'Was Maria Elena at the eatery?'

'I looked in. Beulah was feedin' 'em.'

Elsworth went to lean on a wagon wheel as he gazed straight ahead. 'We got to get her hid.'

'How, with Alvarado and his possemen pokin' and pryin'?'

'I'll think of somethin'.'

Rufe stood up frowning. 'You know what an albatross is?' he asked.

'A what?'

'It's a bird. When I was a button my ma told me about some feller who had an albatross around his neck. It brought him all sorts of bad luck. You'n me

got a pair of albatrosses. I'm goin' back to the store.
You better work up a good story for when Alvarado
comes.'

On the walk back, Rufe had to pass the eatery
again. This time the lawmen weren't inside they were
sitting on an old bench out front. Alvarado nodded
as he said, 'Beulah Bell's crankier'n I remember her,
an' her daughter don't talk nor smile. Like a damned
In'ian.'

Rufe watched the men from Angelina depart to
look after their mounts, entered the café and got a
shock. Maria Elena looked straight at him from
behind the counter where she was stacking three
soiled plates. Beulah poked her head out of the cooking area and squinted. 'Well, what're you starin' at?
You never saw a dark-skinned half-breed before?
Didn't I tell you my man was an In'ian? She's my
daughter. Her name's Flower. Filaria Flower.'

Rufe didn't go to the counter. He was intrigued by
the dark skin and the braided black hair. Beulah
came forward, leaned an' said, 'Tannin' dye.
Alvarado looked at her, asked her name an' was
surprised when I said she was my daughter.'

Rufe finally eased down at the counter looking
steadily at Beulah. 'How in the hell. . . ?'

'I saw 'em come in from the pass. From what Maria
Elena told me I figured they'd be lookin' for her.
Rufe, she needs friends like she's unlikely to ever
need 'em again in her life.'

Rufe leaned forward as he addressed the younger
woman. 'Coffee.'

She almost smiled. 'Black; I remember,' and went
beyond the old blanket to the kitchen.

After she was gone, Beulah leaned down and

spoke so quietly Rufe had to concentrate to catch the words. 'I never had chil'run. I always wanted 'em. I don't know why, me'n my man just never made any, an' we tried.' She straightened back slightly but did not speak louder.

'She's my daughter. I wanted young'uns. My man wanted boys. I never told him I wanted girls.' Her voice resumed its normal harshness. 'That danged lawman'll take her out of the canyon over my dead body. Rufe, I finally done it. I finally got a daughter.'

Beulah lowered her voice again. 'Did she tell you why her'n her man tried to rob the store down at Angelina?'

'She said they had no money.'

'They didn't have. They spent all they got from two other store robberies down near the Reservation. They needed fresh horses, grub an' he busted into old Kemp's store down yonder because they was desperate an' in a hurry.'

'In a hurry?'

Beulah nodded without speaking because Maria Elena appeared with Rufe's black java. Beulah stood aside with arms crossed watching Rufe. Clearly, if he'd attempted to speak she was prepared to cut him off and, as he was sipping coffee, she told Maria Elena she'd better return to the kitchen and make sure the elk roast in the oven wasn't burning.

After Maria Elena left, Rufe arose, put a five-cent piece beside the empty cup and turned to leave when Beulah stopped him. 'I meant what I said, Rufus . . . over my dead body. She's what I've wanted for thirty years.'

Rufe thought of going back to the freighter camp to tell Jim what Beulah had said and how she had

disguised Maria Elena, but the three lawmen from
Angelina were coming from the direction of the
public corrals where their horses were feeding. They
saw him about the same time he saw them, entered
the store, found a customer examining woollen long
johns and went to wait on the man. It was Jim
Elsworth who looked up holding a pair of red long
johns when the marshal and his companions came
in.

Alvarado came to the counter, considered the
underwear Elsworth was holding and said, 'A tad
early for long johns isn't it?' and genially smiled, as
Jim put the underwear back in their box.

Alvarado asked Elsworth to come outside, he'd
like to talk to him. Jim stole a glance at Rufe, turned
and followed the lawman out of the store.

The lawman had left his companions out where
they had tracked the other loose horse. They were to
meet him in the canyon. He considered two old men
herding some milk goats as he spoke. 'Holser's in
that new grave, isn't he?'

Elsworth could answer truthfully. 'Yes.'

Alvarado faced around. 'You buried him?'

Jim's reply was blunt. 'Mister, Wayne Holser'n me
trail drove, rode rough stock, partnered for a couple
of years.'

Alvarado said, 'Like brothers?'

Jim Elsworth nodded.

'An' when he was hurt he come lookin' for his old
partner?'

'No. I hadn't seen Wayne in a long time.'

'But he knew where you were?'

'No . . . I just stumbled onto him.'

'With his woman too?'

Jim was beginning to fidget. 'He's dead. He died—'

'I know where someone died. Up yonder in the high country. With mule tracks, some bloody rags; you found your old partner an' brought him down here where he died.'

'He died in his camp up yonder. I brought him back for a decent burial.'

'And the woman with you?'

Elsworth coloured, he had been coming to this point throughout the questioning. Now he said, 'You're the manhunter. You saw his grave. That ends it, mister.'

Alvarado had to recognize the signs of irritability, but neither his voice nor attitude changed. 'Something you should know,' he told the freighter. 'Your old partner an' his woman robbed a store in the Reservation country an' robbed another store coupla days' ride south of Angelina. The last time a feller got shot. Your friend shot the storekeeper when he reached for a gun in a drawer.'

Elsworth's anger passed. He looked steadily at the town marshal. 'You sure it was Wayne? He never shot anyone when I rode with him an' we got into our share of trouble in trail towns.'

'It was him,' Alvarado said. 'The woman held their horses. That's what she did every time. She's as guilty as he was.'

A dowdy, older woman brushed between them on her way into the store. They gave ground. Alvarado's gaze followed her. 'Cranky old witch.' He cleared his throat, spat and addressed Jim Elsworth again. 'There's a bounty on 'em both. Your old partner did a foolish thing the last time he robbed a store. On his way out he grabbed a mail sack . . . you know what that means? The mail is gov'ment property. When someone steals mail sacks the US Federal Marshals take up the trail. What I don't know is whether your partner knew US marshals was after him or not, but he was hurryin' when he tried robbin' the store in Angelina.'

Jim Elsworth's gaze did not leave the town marshal's face. He knew Wayne Holser had botched the store robbery in Angelina; what neither Holser nor Maria Elena had mentioned was that there had been other robberies.

Jim was turning back toward the store when he said, 'If you expect me to help you, don't. All we did was bury Wayne. If you don't think he's in that grave, dig him up.'

In the store, two people were waiting, Rufe Malone and Beulah Bell. They watched him come inside expressionless and solidly silent. They didn't move nor speak when he sat on the bench looking at them. 'Wayne robbed other places. Him an' Maria Elena.' Elsworth paused. 'He robbed the mail. Alvarado said there'll be federal marshals lookin' for him.'

Beulah responded in her point-blank, harsh way. 'What can they do? He's buried.'

'They want Maria Elena. She held their horses.'

For a moment Beulah was silent and when she eventually did speak she reiterated what she'd said to Rufe, 'They take her over my dead body!' and stamped out of the store.

Rufe jerked his head. Jim Elsworth followed him to the unkempt little office where Rufe leaned to dig out a half-bottle of light tan whiskey. He took a couple of swallows first then handed the freighter the bottle. When Elsworth handed it back he ran a soiled cuff across his mouth, blew out a flammable breath and spoke.

'Wayne was an outlaw for Chris' sake. He robbed stores; Gawd knows what else he did.' Jim sank on to the only chair. 'It don't make sense. Wayne wasn't that kind of a feller.'

Rufe put the bottle away, straightened around and said, 'Your old partner's not the trouble. You know that, don't you?'

The freighter dumbly nodded.

'Beulah did a good job of turnin' a Messican woman into an In'ian woman. . . . Jim, there's bound to have been other folks eat at Beulah's place. If they saw Maria Elena before she become an In'ian, they're goin' to wonder. Sooner or later, Alvarado or some damned lawman'll hear about the change.'

Elsworth dumbly nodded again. He was one of those people who did not recover fast from shock. Eventually he arose from the bench and was looking out into the sun-bright roadway when he spoke. 'Wayne a common gawddamned outlaw?'

Rufe spoke curtly. 'Forget Wayne. No one's goin' to bother him. It's you'n me an' the girl we got to worry about.'

Rufe leaned down on the counter in thought. He broke a lengthy silence by saying, 'What's past is past. We did what she wanted. He's under six feet of dirt which leaves her – an' us, wanted for helpin' to hide her from the law.'

Elsworth returned to the bench. 'I never had much time for women, an' for the life of me I never dreamt I'd be up to my gullet in trouble over one.'

Rufe was a practical man. He brushed his friend's

last statement aside when he said, 'Forget your
friend. Think of us. You never figured you'd be in
trouble over a woman: partner, I never figured I'd be
in trouble with the law. 'Specially the kind US
marshals deal in. Now then, quit whinin' an' think.
How in hell do we weasel out of this mess?'

Instead of replying, the freighter arose and walked
out of the store into mid-morning sun-glare, turned
southward and passed from the storekeeper's sight.

Rufe said, 'Son of a bitch!' and went to his cubbyhole office for another pull on the bottle. When he
returned out front, a cowman named Will Hobart
was drumming on the counter. He straightened,
turned and wagged his head. 'What you got back
there? Whiskey, a poke of gold or a woman? Last few
times I been in here I couldv'e stole half your inventory. Rufe, folks don't like to have to come to a store
an' wait.'

Rufe went behind the counter. He had known the
older man since coming into the canyon. They were
acquaintances not friends. Will Hobart was not a
friendly person.

Rufe said, 'What'll you have?'

'Some Mule Shoe tobacco, a tin of cow salve an' a
couple of them brass lariat hondos.'

While Rufe was getting the old cowman's requirements, Hobart casually said, 'You met them two US
deputy marshals?'

Rufe put the purchases on the counter, ignored
the cowman as he dug out silver coins from a long
leather purse and said, 'What deputy marshals?'

Hobart made no attempt to reply for as long as was
required to put several silver coins on the counter
and recount them. As he was putting the purse back

into a pocket he said, 'Two young fellers. When I met 'em they was talkin' to Carter Alvarado, that town marshal from Angelina.'

'How do you know they was federal marshals?'

Hobart put an almost pitying look on Rufe. 'Because they got them little round badges on their shirts. The kind that got US Deputy Marshal wrote on 'em. Did I count out the money right?'

Rufe nodded without looking at the coins. 'Just right, Will.'

As Hobart was gathering up his purchases he mumbled something about a person who didn't know ciphers very well was never sure and left the store.

Rufe considered another trip to the cubby-hole office, decided he'd wait instead, because sooner or later the strangers would pay him a visit, and he was right.

But before that happened, Maria Elena came pecking on the back door. When he let her in she said, 'Beulah told me . . .'

'Woman,' Rufe exploded, 'why didn't you tell us you'n your man robbed other stores an' stole a mail sack?' He didn't give her a chance to speak. 'Do you know what robbin' the mail means? There's federal lawmen lookin' for you'n Wayne Holser.'

She finally had a chance to speak. 'Beulah said she knows an old trapper who lives out a ways. She said you know him too, and maybe for a few days I should stay out there.'

'Does Beulah know you'n Wayne Holser robbed other stores an' stole a mail sack?'

'I told her. That's why she thinks I should go stay with that old man for a spell. He's a squawman. His woman died years back. Maybe you know him, his name is Bert Freeman.'

Rufe knew Freeman. The old cuss had an unpaid bill at the store which stretched over almost a year.

'Will you take me out there?'

Rufe fidgeted. He didn't want to meet any US deputy marshals but doing what Maria Elena and Beulah Bell wanted him to do would put him a long ways from the store and, like it or not, he had to be around when the federal lawmen came calling.

He said, 'Go tell Jim to take you out yonder. Right now I can't do it.'

5

Three More Reasons to Sweat

Rufe went to the freighter camp. Estralita, Jim's riding mule and another mule, grey as a badger with age, were gone. He went to the eatery. Beulah confirmed that Elsworth had taken Maria Elena out yonder. She also said, 'For a plugged *centavo* I would have poisoned 'em.'

'Poisoned who?'

'Them two smart-aleck deputy US lawmen. They'd talked to Alvarado. Rufe, this mess is gettin' stickier by the minute. Why don't they just leave her alone?'

Rufe said, 'Get me a cup of coffee an' fortify it.'

Beulah didn't move. 'If they try to take her. . . .'

'I know; over your dead body. They'll find her, federals are like 'coon dogs.'

'I should have poisoned 'em.'

Rufe arose to depart. 'Don't talk like that. We got enough damned trouble. What if Bert won't take her in?'

'He will; the old bastard owes me money. An' she's pretty. I told her not to turn her back on the old rascal.'

'Beulah, Bert Freeman's got to be eighty-five.'

'He's a ball-bearing man ain't he?'

Jim Elsworth returned on the second moonless night, came to the back door of the store and when Rufe opened it Jim pushed past, entered the office, sat on the only chair and said, 'I gave the old hermit two silver dollars. He's dirtier'n I remember. Maria Elena told him with me standin' there that she'd make a stone ring an' cook outside. She said his cabin smelled like a boar's nest.'

'I thought Estralita was the only mule that can be rode.'

'Old Sam can be rode. Not reined but rode. He's almost thirty years old. He'd put up with a catamount on his back. Rufe?'

'What?'

'You met the federals yet?'

'No, but you can bet your mules they'll be along.'

Rufe would have won that wager hands down. The following morning they entered the store as Rufe was using some bound turkey feathers to dust shelves.

It was possible to recognize new hands from old ones. These two wore their badges in plain sight. Deputy US marshals who were long in the tooth were more discreet.

Rufe's visitors were young, most likely somewhere in their twenties. Both were tall. One had brown eyes, the other one's eyes were blue. The brown-eyed one introduced himself and his companion as he shoved out a hand. 'My name's Wes Mason. This here is Eli Poyer. We're federal marshals lookin' for a Messican woman named Maria Elena Quintera.'

If Rufe had ever heard Maria Elena's last name he

couldn't recall it but he nodded. 'Glad to meet you gents.'

The brown-eyed lawman named Wes Mason asked a question. 'You know this woman, Mister Malone?'

Rufe's answer was cryptic. 'I've met her.'

'What can you tell us about her.'

'Not much. You're interested?'

'We got a federal warrant for her arrest.'

'What did she do?'

'Her an' a feller named Wayne Holser committed a string of robberies. The last one was down in Angelina. As they was runnin' for it Holser got shot. Marshal Alvarado found where Holser camped. He died up there. Alvarado said he's buried down here.'

Rufe nodded about that and Mason's next question could have been anticipated. 'You knew Holser?'

'Nope; met him just before he died.'

'And brought him back here to be buried?'

'Well, yes. I'd have done as much for anyone.'

Mason smiled a little. 'Sure. Most of us would. Where is the woman?'

Rufe's reply was neither a lie nor the truth. 'I haven't seen her lately. I'd guess, knowin' the law was after her she left the country.'

The blue-eyed man named Eli Poyer spoke for the first time. 'Accordin' to Marshal Alvarado, she was here an' is most likely still here. Would you know anythin' about that?'

Rufe bristled. 'I told you all I know. If she's still here I got no idea where she'd be. This is a small settlement. Folks know each other like a family. Besides, they wouldn't knowingly hide an outlaw, not even a female one.'

Mason spoke again. 'You think she's gone?'

'Yes, sir, I do. Would you stay here if you knew the law was lookin' for you?'

If Mason had intended to reply he didn't get the chance. Two old men entered the store, nodded around and put a scrap of paper on the counter in front of Rufe. He nodded to them and addressed the lawman. 'These here are the Martin brothers. They're deef an' dumb.'

When Rufe returned to the counter to put the items on the list in front of the pair of old men the federal officers were gone. He was back dusting shelves when the cowman named Hobart walked in, not to make purchases but to say, 'What the hell is goin' on, Rufe? The other night my dogs raised hell so I took a rifle out expectin' to find varmints. Two riders on mules went past It was too dark to make out much but I'd know Jim Elsworth's mules if I was blindfolded. They went west. The onliest place beyond up the canyon is where that old rascal Bert Freeman lives. Rufe, one of them mule riders was a female woman.'

'You said you couldn't make out much.'

'I couldn't, but one of my dogs, Beauty, barks different around women than she does around men. . . . Rufe, what's goin' on?'

Two interruptions in one day was a little much for the storekeeper so his answer was curt. 'Why ask me?'

'Because,' the older man answered sharply, 'nothin' happens in the canyon that don't get talked about in your store. Who was them mule riders?'

Will Hobart had a reputation for doggedness. It was clearly his intention not to leave the store until he got satisfactory answers. Rufe said, 'Go ask Jim, if it was him.'

Hobart answered curtly. 'I did, an' he lied like a soldier. He said neither him nor his mules left the camp the other night.'

'Then that settles it,' Rufe replied.

'Not by a damned sight. I'm goin' up to Bert's cabin. He might be involved in rustlin' or somethin' as bad. I've lived a few miles from him for twenty years an' I can tell you he's not above gettin' mixed up in some kind of lawlessness.'

Rufe considered the square-jawed, hard-eyed, old stockman. Hobart was more stubborn than a Missouri mule. He was also cranky enough to stir up trouble. Rufe said, 'Will, those two federal marshals are lookin' for a Messican girl.'

'What did she do?'

'Helped rob some stores.'

'By herself?'

'No, she had a partner.'

'They're lookin' for him too?'

'He's in the fresh grave out at the burial ground so they want the woman.'

'She shoot anyone?'

'No. She held the horses.'

Hobart considered, his brow puckered and his gaze at Rufe showed temper. 'She's holed-up at Bert's place?'

Rufe nodded.

'Well now, that's no place for a lady. I'll take her down to my place. Are you goin' to tell them federal lawmen where she is?'

'Not on your life.'

'Sweet on her, are you?'

Rufe coloured. 'No! I wish I'd never seen her.'

'How about Jim, is he sweet on her?'

'Ask him. What he does isn't none of my business.'

Hobart stood briefly gazing at Rufe and, as he was turning to leave, he said, 'She shouldn't be left alone with Bert. He's not only bad, he's downright evil. I'll take her down to my place. Mind you, no matter who asks, you got no idea where she's at.'

Rufe stopped the older man in his tracks. 'Will, you're borrowin' trouble.'

Hobart snorted. 'You know what my middle name is? It's trouble.'

When the cowman left, Rufe returned to Elsworth's camp to relate the events of his meeting with Will Hobart and Jim got indignant. 'Why'd you tell the old bastard anythin' at all?'

'Because I don't like the idea of her bein' in that isolated canyon alone with Bert Freeman. Also, because if the law comes sniffin' around, Freeman'd sell her for the bounty an' Will Hobart'd shoot the legs out from under 'em if they come into his yard with those badges.'

'Does Beulah know?' Jim asked.

'You can explain it to her,' Rufe said, and left the camp. Women! A man couldn't even do a good deed for 'em without landing in trouble up to his butt!

Town Marshal Alvarado and his pair of townsmen left Hell's Canyon; Alvarado had a settlement to look after. Moreover, with a pair of federal lawmen in the canyon whose authority exceeded his, he was content to terminate his search. He had told them everything he knew and was confident they would make good use of it.

No one missed Carter Alvarado, certainly not Beulah Bell who came storming down to the general store with fully ruffled feathers. 'Why in hell,' she

demanded, 'did you go to all the trouble of sneakin'
Maria Elena away from here in the damned night,
then talk to them damned lawmen?'

Rufe was just as roiled. 'Because Will Hobart's
goin' to take her down to his place where she'll be
safer than up that canyon with Bert Freeman.'

'Will Hobart! That old devil's meaner'n a bear
with a sore behind.'

'Beulah, we need every friend we can get. Will
Hobart'll run off those federal lawmen if they come
snoopin' around. Maybe you have faith in Bert
Freeman, but if it was up to me I'd prefer Will
Hobart to a hundred Bert Freemans.'

'That's not the issue, Rufe. Keep this up an' everyone in the canyon will know who she is an' that the
law's after her. It was a secret but it sure as hell won't
be one now.'

Beulah would have wrung her hands if she'd been
the hand-wringing type. 'She never said a word to me.
And when I found her bed hadn't been slept in. . . .'

'You made the arrangement with Bert Freeman.'

Beulah went to the bench, sat down and looked
almost pleadingly at Rufe. 'She's my daughter.'

Rufe understood, not entirely but well enough.
When next he spoke his voice was softer. 'Beulah, as
far as I know no one's ever rode into Will Hobart's
yard braced for trouble that they'd leave it faster'n
they entered it. As for this mess being a secret. . . .'
Rufe shook his head. 'Not in Hell's Canyon. There
aren't no secrets. She needs supporters, every blessed
one she can get.'

'Maybe I'll ride out there,' Beulah said, and Rufe
shook his head. 'For now leave it be. Old Hobart'll
likely run you off too.'

'How?'

'Sic his dogs on you for openers. Beulah, she's in better hands. I know Will Hobart as well as anyone does. If I had a choice to make for someone to take her side Hobart'd be my first choice.'

After Beulah returned to her eatery and Rufe was again whisking with his turkey-feather duster, he was interrupted and this time there were three of them, dusty, weathered men who had clearly been days in the saddle.

One of them was big-boned and heavily muscular. He said his name was Evan Whittier. His companions, also large-boned, powerfully-put-together men were Evan Whittier's brothers, Herbert and Jubal.

No one offered a hand as Evan, obviously the spokesman, said, 'Folks back yonder in Angelina told us an outlaw named Wayne Holser and his woman come up this way. He's a feller about our height, not as heavy with . . .'

Rufe interrupted. 'You want to see him? Walk out to the cemetery. He's in the only new grave out there.'

Evan Whittier was shocked. 'The hell. He's dead?'

Rufe nodded. 'They don't get any deader. Didn't they tell you down in Angelina the marshal shot him?'

Evan nodded. 'They told us, but a man ridin' a runnin' horse don't stay atop it if he's hurt bad.'

'He died. I told you where he's buried.'

'What about his accomplice, the Messican woman?'

Rufe told a marginal truth and a marginal untruth. 'I got no idea where she is, but there are two deputy federal marshals lookin' for her.'

'They're here, in the canyon?'

'As far as I know. Last time I saw 'em they were standin' about where you're standin'.'

Evan Whittier jerked his head and they exited from Rufe's store. He watched them go with a sinking, leaden sensation in his stomach.

That evening, with the store locked for the day, Rufe was in his cubbyhole office engrossed with one of the chores he detested about storekeeping, inventorying his stock that needed replenishing. In most settlements, merchants maintained a running inventory; in Hellsville's general store trade did not warrant anything that businesslike and efficient. The store paid its way but just barely. If he'd owned a store like Art Kemp's establishment in Angelina he'd have maybe thrown in the sponge or sold out. In his lifetime he'd done several things including operating a saloon; he'd have done that in the canyon if there had have been sufficient trade to warrant it. In isolated places like Hell's Canyon folks made their own corn squeezings.

He finished with the list of needed replacements and arose to blow down the lamp mantle when someone rapped on the rear door.

He went to see who was out there with a sense of relief. As long as Rufe Malone lived he would detest anything that had to do with bookkeeping or inventorying.

The caller was Jim Elsworth and, as he'd done on previous occasions, he brushed past Rufe, went into the darkened office, sat down and said, 'Light that lamp. I got somethin' to tell you.'

Rufe lighted the lamp, turned and waited. It was a short wait.

'There's three fellers lookin' for her an' they're not lawmen, they're the sons of the storekeeper down near the Reservation that got shot by Wayne when he was robbin' the store.'

Rufe let go a sigh. 'The Whittiers.'

It was Elsworth's turn to show surprise. 'You met 'em?'

'This afternoon in the store. I told 'em where your partner's buried. They knew Alvarado had shot him. Jim, him bein' dead would satisfy me, but the Whittier boys, like them two federal lawmen, want Maria Elena. Did you know her last name was Quintera?'

Jim ignored the question. 'There's somethin' else. Beulah told me Maria Elena left Bert Freeman to go down to Will Hobart's place.'

Rufe drily said, 'Yeah. She's better off with Hobart.'

Jim's response was unsettling. 'Freeman come to town lookin' for Beulah. She wasn't at the eatery.'

Rufe nodded about that too. 'She said she was goin' out to the Hobart place.'

'Rufe, Bert had been drinkin'. He was upset Maria Elena went with Hobart. Accordin' to Bert, Hobart come into his canyon leadin' a saddled horse, threw down on Bert an' took her away with him. Bert's been tellin' that to everybody who'd listen. You know what that means?'

Rufe knew. He stood leaning against his desk, arms folded, looking steadily at Elsworth. 'Them Whittier boys is out for blood, them federals is after her hide too. Sure as I'm standin' here between them two factions they'll run into Freeman an' you can guess the rest. They'll go to the Hobart place, separately or all five of 'em. You want me to guess the rest of it? Will Hobart'll fight 'em.'

Elsworth loosened in the chair, pushed out his legs and swore. 'Whatever happens out there, Freeman'll tell 'em how Maria Elena came to be at his place; they'll trace that back to Beulah an' to us.'

'You had to bring your old partner back here an' bury him.' The freighter let that pass. 'We got to go out there.'

'Out where?'

'To Hobart's place an' we got to do it right now, tonight, before the sons of that storekeeper an' those US deputies get there. We got to get her away and hide her.'

'Where, for Chris'sake?'

'I got no idea, but on the ride out there we can figure somethin'.'

'Jim, I'm about ready to hand her over to the law.'

Elsworth shot up off the chair. 'Well, I ain't. There's three of them Whittiers an' two greenhorn deputy marshals. They'll take her from the federals.'

Rufe continued to study his friend. 'Let me ask you a question, Jim. Are you sweet on Maria Elena whatever-her-last-name-is?'

Elsworth hung fire before saying. 'Did you ever see a woman get hung? Neither have I, but I'll be damned if it's goin' to happen.'

Rufe didn't move. What had started out as an act of common decency had evolved into something he could not have anticipated; the longer he leaned there looking at his friend the more that sinking feeling behind his belt worsened. Nor did it help when Elsworth abruptly said, 'She's pretty as a speckled bird. She's decent and stood by Wayne when he got shot an' was dyin'. I'm crowdin' my late forties. She's the decentest woman I've ever run across.'

'You *are* sweet on her.'

Elsworth's reply was short. 'I'm goin' out there. You can stay here and mind your store.'

'You'll likely get yourself killed. Them Whittiers looked to me like fellers who'd wrestle a cougar with their bare hands.'

Elsworth started for the dark, short passageway that led to the rear door. As he was moving he said, 'It's not just for her, it's also for Wayne.'

Rufe growled, 'Like hell it is. Wayne's dead. No one can do anythin' to him. . . . Get Estralita, I'll meet you out back in fifteen minutes.'

Jim Elsworth stopped and turned as though he meant to say something. Rufe didn't give him the chance. 'An' bring your Winchester. My guess is that no one'll have got out there and won't show up until daylight. *Get your damned mule!*'

6

A Long Cold Night

It was chilly as it always was in low places where sunshine stopped giving warmth in late afternoon. There was an infrequent scattering of distant lights. Coal oil for lamps was expensive, candles were cheaper. They were also frustrating to see by so folks retired early.

Rufe's foul mood lingered. Several times when Jim, astride Estralita, tried to break silences all he got in return were grunts.

When the chill turned to downright cold, the riders turned up jacket collars and pulled their heads down into their coats like turtles. For some time now Rufe had relived his existence for the past few weeks so naturally his foul mood lingered. Up until this night there had been considerable talk mixed with increased exasperation, but now, colder than a witch's bosom, with a saddle gun in its boot under his right saddle fender and a shellbelted, holstered Colt around his middle, it was obvious to him that the time for palavering was over and serious trouble was up ahead where a tiny pinprick of light showed at the Hobart home place.

He came out of his gloom long enough to say, 'He's got dogs.'

Jim Elsworth's reply was brusque. 'I never knew folks who lived out a ways who didn't have 'em.'

Rufe squinted at the pinprick of light. 'Hobart's likely to shoot first an' talk afterwards.'

Jim was sanguine about this too. 'Havin' Maria Elena at his place I'd act the same. Why did he want to take her in? Did you tell him he'd be askin' for trouble?'

'I told him. He said trouble was his middle name. Jim, we'd better sound off.'

'Too far yet.'

Rufe stood in his stirrups, cupped both hands and shouted. As he settled back, Jim said, 'I don't hear the dogs.'

A hundred feet further along the barking started. What Rufe noticed was that the lamp in the house abruptly went out. He said, 'We better get down an' lead the animals.'

It was sound advice even though the distance to the yard was still considerable. As they walked, Jim said, 'We got to have a strategy worked out before them lawmen and the Whittiers get here.'

This time it was Rufe who sounded un-hurried. 'Plenty of time for strategy. We'll be lucky to get inside.'

As they walked into the yard three dogs challenged them. Of the three only one had attack instincts, the other two were content to make noise. The third dog, all black except for four white toes, left off barking, allowed the men leading horses to pass, then tried sneaking up behind them to bite.

The black dog made a mistake. He was skulking behind in order to have cover until he could reach the men. Estralita neither looked back to aim nor bunched up when she kicked. The black dog yelped as he rolled over several times, got back on to his feet and headed for the barn perfectly willing to leave challenging to the younger, less warlike dogs.

Rufe and the freighter were passing the wide door-less barn opening when a man spoke from the barn's pitch-black interior.

'What do you want? Stop where you are. Turn your backs to me. Good. Now shuck them sidearms. Don't talk, just shuck 'em.'

Rufe dropped his belt-gun, looked at Jim and softly said, 'I told you.'

The invisible man spoke again. 'Who are you?'

Elsworth answered. 'He's Rufe Malone from the settlement store an' I'm Jim Elsworth. I freight. Are you Will Hobart?'

Instead of replying, the man in barn darkness emerged. He remained behind his captives, but the rough edge was off his voice when he replied, 'I'm Hobart. What're you two doin' out here?'

Rufe spoke before Jim could. 'You mind if we go inside? It's cold out here.'

Rufe got a curt answer. 'I mind. Answer my question.'

Rufe answered. 'There's a pair of deputy US marshals lookin' for Maria Elena an' there's three sons of a feller that got shot down near the Reservation when her and Wayne Holser robbed a store. Will, it's our guess them five'll be lookin' for her in the morning. The federal lawmen got a warrant. They'll take her back with 'em, but those three other fellers look like rangemen to me an' unless I'm wrong they're the hangin' type. It was their pa got shot.'

'Killed?'

'I don't know. We didn't even know Wayne Holser robbed other stores besides Kemp's place in Angelina which is where Carter Alvarado shot him, an' after he died me'n Jim buried him. Now can we go inside?'

Will Hobart put up his weapon and wordlessly led the way. Two tail-wagging young dogs went as far as the porch with them. The black dog was already under the porch.

The parlour had a large stone fireplace with split cord wood stacked on one side and a bucket of fat-wood kindling on the other side. The furnishings were typical of a single man; they were sparse, worn and completely unpretentious.

Hobart relighted the lamp. Maria Elena stood in the kitchen doorway as still and silent as a wooden Indian.

Hobart rummaged in a deep drawer, brought forth jolt glasses and a bottle of whiskey as clear as water. As he set those things on a round oaken table he said, 'That'll hold you until I stoke up the fire,' and went to feed fat-wood kindling and as it blazed up he fed in quarter rounds of dry fir. The fire brightened the room more than the lamp did.

Jim told Maria Elena who was looking for her. She accepted this impassively and did not speak until Will Hobart said, 'You never told me you'n your feller robbed a string of stores.'

Her answer was explicit. 'Would it have made any

difference? I didn't know US marshals were after us.'

Rufe cleared that up gruffly. 'When your partner took a mail sack he guaranteed they'd be after both of you. The US mail is gov'ment property an' federal lawmen don't take it kindly when someone steals it.'

Maria Elena said, 'There was no money in the letters, just letters and only a dozen or so of them.'

Rufe went to ease down in a leather chair and while unbuttoning his coat he looked steadily at the woman.

'Now you know. What happened to the letters an' the sack?'

'I used them to get a fire going up where you found us.'

Will Hobart poured three glasses and handed them around. After downing his jolt he said, 'Five of 'em?' and when Rufe nodded he also said, 'There won't be time to get help if they show up in the morning, otherwise I could get the Houston boys, neighbours about five, six miles from here. Maybe I'd ought to try anyway.'

Jim downed whiskey and coughed before saying, 'Mister Hobart, this is your place. If they come, Rufe'n I can't rough 'em like you could. We're just visitors.'

Maria Elena held up a hand for silence. The dogs began barking and this time it was all three. Someone loudly swore and Will Hobart started for the door. Rufe was arising when he said, 'Don't open it. The fire'll background you.'

Hobart halted with his left hand on the latch. The profanity out in the night got stronger. Hobart looked over his shoulder.

'Beulah! I'd know that voice anywhere.' He

yanked the door open and simultaneously yelled at the dogs, moved to one side and as the dowdy, greying woman entered carrying a long twin-barrelled shotgun and wearing a holstered Colt around her coat, she said, 'Will Hobart, if them dogs bite me I'll slit your pouch an' pull your leg through it!'

Hobart made a flinty smile, closed the door and while gazing at the shotgun asked Beulah a question. 'Where's your horse?'

Her answer was in character. 'You know I don't own a horse.'

'You walked all the way?' Hobart asked.

'Every blessed foot an' walkin' was never my favourite way of gettin' around.' She swung her attention to Maria Elena. 'Any of 'em bothered you? Leastways you got clear of Bert. I wouldn't have sent you to him except his place is a natural hideout.' She considered Rufe and Jim Elsworth. 'You aren't in the best company now, neither.'

She went to the table, filled a jolt glass and downed its contents, wiped her mouth on a coat sleeve and said, 'It's gettin' colder out there than a witch's buzzom. Well, where are the US marshals?'

Jim explained about the Whittiers; ended his remark saying he and Rufe didn't think the lawmen or the rangemen would show up before sunrise, and Beulah went to an old leather sofa, sat down, pulled off her knit cap, leaned the scattergun aside and scowled at Will Hobart. 'I expect you'd charge me like I been chargin' you for somethin' to eat.'

Hobart went to poke at the fire. Maria Elena went into the kitchen. The men could hear the pair of women talking in there. Hobart considered the storekeeper and the mule-man. 'Now, what'll we do with her?' he asked and got a quick reply from Jim Elsworth.

'Whatever she wants us to do with her. You know how long a walk that is?'

Hobart ignored the questions and addressed Rufe. 'I get the feelin' you're more worried about them Whittiers than you are about the federal lawmen.'

Rufe replied honestly. 'I am. I know rangemen. I was one for some years. What they can't shoot they hang.'

Hobart's response to that was given in a calm, steady tone of voice. 'I don't think we'll allow that. Have another jolt. Elsworth; do your mules kick?'

'No. Why?'

'Because one of us got to go stall an' feed them and Rufe's horse, an' since I never trusted mules it seems to me you can do that chore.'

As Jim arose so did Rufe. He said, 'I'll go with him.'

After the two men from the settlement left the house Will Hobart went to lean in the kitchen doorway regarding Beulah Bell. He was curious. 'That girl don't look Messican to me. She looks In'ian.'

Beulah replied while slicing coarse-grain bread. 'She's my daughter. Her pa, my husband, was a full blood.'

'Is that a fact? Then that'd explain why her an' her man come to the canyon. She knew her ma was here.'

Neither of the women spoke. If that satisfied Hobart they were willing for that to be.

He had a question for Maria Elena. 'That store-keeper your friend shot, he died?'

Maria Elena had no way of knowing. She said they

had jumped on their horses and lit out in a belly-down run after the robbery and shooting. She did not know whether the storekeeper had been killed outright or not.

Beulah had an opinion about that. 'If he wasn't killed why would his sons take to the trail the way they did?'

Hobart returned to the parlour where he listened and when two sets of boots reached the porch he went to open the door and a wisp of cold air came in with Rufe and the freighter.

Hobart said, 'Any sign?' and Jim shook his head as he sank down in a chair and dropped his hat beside it. 'No, but daylight's comin',' he said. 'If we don't get all five of 'em sure as grass is green we'll get at least two. Mister Hobart, you know anythin' about buckin' the law?'

'I know my rights an' that includes trespassers, badge heavy or not.'

'They got a warrant. You resist an' they'll arrest you too.'

'They won't be gettin' a virgin, I've been arrested before. Now let me ask you lads a question. How far will you go to prevent any of those gents from gettin' Maria Elena?'

Before Rufe could answer Jim spoke with sufficient fervour to make Rufe turn and stare. Elsworth said, 'As far as I got to go. Like Beulah said . . . over my dead body.'

Will Hobart studied Elsworth over a lengthy period of silence, then changed the subject as he faced Rufe Malone.

Whatever he might have said was interrupted by barking dogs. Hobart blew down the lamp mantle leaving the only light in the parlour coming from the fireplace.

Rufe went to the door, cracked it several inches while Jim Elsworth went through the kitchen, blowing out candles as he passed and carefully used a slight lifting pressure as he opened the door. The door didn't squeak. It didn't squeak without being opened cautiously.

Hobart disappeared down a dingy hallway. The only sound except for the dogs was made when he opened a window that hadn't been opened in a 'coon's age and resisted being opened now.

The dogs were caterwauling in the vicinity of the barn, which made sense to Rufe. Whoever was out there an hour or so ahead of sunrise would look for, and find, ridden animals which would warn him how many men might be in the house.

If he could have made a choice he would have wished whoever was out there would be the pair of boyish federal deputies.

Jim came back through the kitchen where he paused to briefly converse with the women then groped his way in Rufe's direction.

'Didn't see a soul, but they're out there. Sounds like they're at the barn.'

None of this was particularly troubling to Rufe who had already made his conclusions. They parallelled what Elsworth had just said, so he turned and spoke quietly.

'If it's the Whittiers I'd guess they know about burnin' folks out.'

Will Hobart returned to the parlour in time to hear Rufe's last statement and his reaction was in keeping with what people said of Will Hobart.

'If they try that an' I catch one, I'll cook his damned bare feet in the fireplace.'

Neither of the settlement men commented, they leaned to catch every sound and were rewarded when a mule brayed and a horse squealed. Most horses tolerated mules, but not all did and from the sounds in the fading darkness someone's riding animal belonged to that minority.

Jim's reaction could have been expected. 'If that damned horse bites my mule I'll skin him alive.'

Rufe ignored that threat as he had ignored Will Hobart's earlier threat about roasting bare feet.

He thought the horse and mule were in adjoining stalls. They kept up their squabbling which masked any other sounds and that annoyed the storekeeper because between the barn and house there was precious little cover for use of stealthy intruders.

Beulah appeared in the parlour with full cheeks and chewing. When she was able she told the uninterested men that a man'd be a fool not to marry Maria Elena for her cooking, and with her back to the kitchen door where Maria Elena was standing, Beulah also said, 'That girl never hurt nobody in her life. All she did was hold the horses.'

Rufe gave Beulah an exasperated look and she returned to the kitchen at the same time Will Hobart growled if whoever was out there waited an hour or so longer the sun would be up and they'd be sitting ducks.

Rufe ignored that too. His peek hole around the edge of the slightly opened door let him see two dark shadows moving down near the barn.

There were two small buildings on the east side of the yard. Either building could have been a storehouse. Whatever their function they provided expert cover for stalkers. He watched the pair of shadows. When one returned to the barn the other sooty silhouette headed for one of the little log buildings in a roundabout fashion.

Hobart spoke abruptly from behind the store-keeper. 'Shoot!'

Rufe didn't raise a gun.

'What the hell was you waitin' for!' Hobart exclaimed.

Rufe twisted to look back as he said, 'I sort of like to know who I'm aimin' at.'

Hobart abruptly turned away muttering under his breath.

Rufe saw the shadowy form fade from sight on the north side of the shed nearly opposite the barn.

The dogs were in a frenzy. The black attack-dog didn't go far from his safe place beneath the porch but the younger dogs did, they both stalked the barn until someone threw something then they joined the older dog closer to the house.

Jim joined Rufe at the door. There was no visible movement. He said, 'That'll be the marshals. They are just naturally careful.'

The shadow in the barn emerged walking toward the house. Rufe beckoned Will Hobart. There were three men at the nearly closed door when the intruder halted a few feet from the porch steps and called out. 'Mister Hobart. . . .'

The older man answered gruffly. 'I'm here. Who are you an' what the hell do you want?'

'I'm Deputy US Marshal Wes Mason. Your neigh-bour Bert Freeman told me you got a Messican woman in there an' I got a federal warrant for her arrest.'

Hobart shouldered Rufe slightly so he could see past into the yard and his retort surprised no one in the house. 'All I got in here, mister, is some friends, an' you're trespassin'.'

'Is the Messican woman in there?'

'Who I got in here is none of your damned business. As far as I know you're some skulkin' outlaw. Get out of my yard before I shoot you.'

The federal deputy marshal turned without another word, walked all the way to the barn and disappeared inside. Jim said, 'Where's the other one?'

Rufe answered. 'Sneakin' up from behind that little house across from the barn.'

Hobart abruptly left the door, passed through the kitchen and told Beulah to stand clear as he cracked the door enough to see out. If there was someone stalking the house from the east side of the yard Hobart would be able to see him when he moved from the northerly shed to the one closer to the house.

The intruder in the barn stepped outside and called again. 'You're defyin' federal law, Mister Hobart, an' that can land you in a heap of trouble.'

Hobart's reply was one Rufe Malone had heard before.

Hobart said, 'Boy, trouble is my middle name. Why didn't you come straight to the house when you rode in, instead of sneakin' around in the dark?'

Mason's next remark was delayed but eventually it came. 'Mister Hobart, send the Messican woman out. If you don't we'll bring in the army.'

Hobart snorted loudly. 'Aren't no soldiers closer'n Fort Seaver, sixty miles from here.'

'We can wait. We'll bottle you up until they get here. Use your head, Hobart. Buckin' the law can set you up to spend the rest of your life in prison. Send her out!'

This time Hobart's reply was offered in four words. 'Come and get her!'

7

Three Strangers

The men at the door were fully occupied. Not until Maria Elena timidly came to tap Rufe's shoulder did they turn. Maria Elena said, 'Beulah's gone.'

After a moment Hobart said, 'What are you talkin' about?' and peered toward the kitchen.

Maria Elena's reply sounded as timid as she was feeling. 'She left the shotgun in the kitchen, went out the back door and said for me not to tell any of you for ten minutes. It's been more'n ten minutes.'

Will Hobart blustered, 'Gone? Gone where? What's she up to, the old witch?'

Maria Elena had told them all she knew. She had no idea where Beulah had gone and when Rufe said, 'To palaver with the lawmen?' Maria Elena shook her head without speaking.

Rufe and Will Hobart went to the kitchen, leaving Jim Elsworth at the door. Hobart picked up the long-barrelled shotgun, broke it, extracted two loads and snapped it closed. As he was leaning the weapon aside he said, 'What in the hell is she. . . . Not hike back to the settlement for help. You don't expect she figures to skulk around an' come up behind them lawmen?'

Rufe's reply was dour. 'She'd get herself killed.'

Maria Elena fled from the room and Jim Elsworth attempted an interception, but she eluded him and Hobart growled for Jim to leave her be, which Jim did.

Rufe returned to the door. There was no sign of the stalking deputy marshal but he didn't expect anything different. Young though the lawman might be, he'd been trained.

False dawn arrived, visibility improved. Sunrise would be another hour or so. Visibility was good, but without sunlight it was sickly grey and cold.

Hobart was in the centre of the parlour when he said, 'What are they waitin' for?'

Elsworth made a guess. 'For us to carry the fight to them. Make targets for 'em.'

The men got a shock. Beulah yelled from the vicinity of the barn. 'Mister Hobart! Rufe an' Jim! Don't do nothin' rash. We're comin' to the house.'

They watched wordlessly as Beulah led off from the barn with the pair of federal lawmen behind her.

Hobart said, 'Good girl. She's bringin' 'em where we can disarm 'em.'

Neither Rufe nor Jim commented. When Beulah started up the porch steps a dog growled from beneath the porch. That was the only sound until she said, 'Well, damn it, open the door!'

Rufe opened it. Beulah led the way to the parlour where she faced around. 'Where's my daughter?'

Will Hobart, with no idea of what she was talking about, stared. Rufe jutted his jaw. 'In one of the back rooms. It upset her bad when you left the house.'

Beulah faced Jim Elsworth. 'Go fetch her. Mister Hobart, this here is Deputy US Marshal Wes Mason.

This here is another federal marshal, Eli Poyer.'

Hobart didn't nod and neither did the younger men.

Jim appeared with Maria Elena trailing him. Beulah opened her arms and Maria Elena went into them. Beulah spoke again. 'This here is my daughter. Her pa was a full blood.'

For several seconds none of the men spoke until the blue-eyed lawman said, 'I've seen Messicans darker'n she is.'

Beulah glared. 'I expect you have, mister, but this ain't one of 'em.'

The dark-eyed marshal turned on Will Hobart. 'If she isn't the Quintera woman why did you refuse to let us in? Why didn't you say who she. . . .'

'Because I don't like trespassers, mister,' Hobart exclaimed. 'Badges or not. I just plain don't tolerate folks trespassin' on my land. You boys get astraddle and get off my land right damned now!'

The lawmen exchanged a long look before Eli Poyer told Maria Elena to face him. When she would have obeyed Beulah hugged her tightly. 'You want me to write it down for you? She's my daughter.'

'What was her pa's name?'

'Buffalo Hump. Dakota pure blood.'

Again the lawmen exchanged a look before the one named Mason started for the door, stopped in the opening and glared at Will Hobart. 'Mister, someday you're goin' to get in trouble up to your neck.'

Rufe braced but Hobart did not say it. He didn't have to, trouble *was* his middle name.

Rufe went out onto the porch to watch the federal deputies ride out of the yard. He could hear Beulah and Will Hobart arguing. Jim came out, scratched and let go a long, ragged sigh.

Rufe continued to watch the distant riders, who now had the sun in their faces, when he said, 'Crazy old woman.'

Jim's response was more charitable. 'It worked, that stain on her face'n arms an' the black braids. Rufe, she out-smarted all of us. Good thing them lawmen didn't have a dodger with her picture on it.'

Beulah bellowed for them to come inside, breakfast was ready.

Will Hobart ate like a horse while the others picked at their food. He was not accustomed to woman-cooked food; living alone and being unable to cook worth a damn made a difference. If there'd been a shoot-out fight he still would have eaten breakfast like a starved wolf.

With the crisis passed, Jim was ready to get back to his camp. Where his animals were concerned Jim Elsworth was a worrier.

Rufe had the store to look after. While it was marginally profitable it was his life and his habit. Aside from those things he was still annoyed. If anyone had asked him about the predicament he had gotten into simply because he believed a dead man deserved a decent burial, Rufe would have bluntly said that if he had it to do over again he might have helped with the decent burial but he wouldn't have raised a hand to help the Messican woman.

After breakfast, Will Hobart and Beulah Bell went down to the barn with the settlement men. Maria Elena came too. She and Jim exchanged looks and while the animals were being rigged out, Jim told

Maria Elena he'd admire to ride out and visit. Her reaction in front of them all was a wistful smile and several barely heard words.

'I would like you to do that. Any time.'

On the ride back with sun-smash in their faces they tipped down hat brims. Rufe searched the land for rooftops while Jim talked of Maria Elena. He said not a word of Beulah's successful ruse.

It was late morning before they drew rein in front of the store. Two women sitting on a nearby bench looked daggers at Rufe which he ignored until he and Jim had briefly pumped hands before Rufe said, 'Good luck.'

After the mule-man had departed and Rufe had unlocked the store, the pair of women came in and Rufe braced for the tongue lashing that never came. One of the shoppers pithily said what Rufe had heard so many times over the years, but particularly lately that he could repeat it in his sleep.

'Folks that owns stores should keep regular schedules. Me'n Mrs Leland been sittin' out there more'n an hour ... I want two pair of red long johns for my husband, an Miz Leland would like to see what you got in winter wool shirts, large size, for her husband.'

Rufe was kept occupied until high noon, about the time people ate. He had no idea whether Beulah had returned yet or not but was starting to leave the store, walk up to the eatery to see, when three large, weathered men blocked his exit, pushed him back and blocked the roadway door. They were unsmiling for an excellent reason.

One of them said, 'You remember us, Mister Storekeeper? We was in day afore yestiddy about a

Messican woman. You recollect?' Rufe went around behind his counter and while leaning down opened an under-counter drawer with two fingers. The drawer held a carton of shells and a pearl-handled, elegantly engraved six-gun that Rufe had taken in payment for a large debt three years earlier.

Evan Whittier stood across the counter. His brothers ambled elsewhere examining shelves and counters where bolt goods were stacked.

Evan said, 'We met them deputy marshals this mornin'. They told us about what happened out yonder. They was satisfied the eatery woman's daughter was a 'breed In'ian.'

Rufe nodded. 'I was out there.'

'So they said. You'n another feller.'

'Jim Elsworth. He's a freighter.'

The burly man nodded. 'Well now, mister, we never told them lawmen the eatery woman don't have a daughter. We talked to folks who been in this canyon as long as she has an' they said she come here alone, opened her eatery, had no husband an' no daughter.'

The pair of meandering Whittiers drifted back and stood with Evan looking impassively at Rufe. The one named Herbert, who seemed slightly younger than the others, softly said, 'Why'd you an' the mule-man ride out there last night?'

Rufe fumbled for an answer and eventually lied. 'To see if Will Hobart was sick. We heard he was.'

The soft-spoken Whittier spoke again. 'You call on sick folks carryin' saddle guns and Colts? What'd you figure, to put him out of his misery?'

Rufe's temper was rising. As he straightened up off the counter he ignored the soft-spoken Whittier and looked directly at Evan Whittier. 'Did you come in here lookin' for trouble?'

Evan answered. 'Don't reach in that drawer, friend. What we come in for was to show you a couple of dodgers.' The burly man drew forth two folded papers, flattened them on the counter facing Rufe and said, 'We're satisfied that one's buried out yonder. Mister Alvarado told us he is. Now then, we didn't show these posters to the lawmen. We was tempted to but if we had they'd've turned around an' come back an' we didn't want that.' Evan Whittier hit the second dodger with a fist. 'Is that the woman, Storekeeper?'

Rufe ignored the dodger when he said, 'You want a piece of advice? Ride out of here an' don't come back.'

Evan Whittier picked up the dodgers, folded them and put them in a pocket. For the first time he showed an expression. He made a bleak small smile. 'That's her, isn't it? Her friend shot our pa in the hip. He won't be able to walk for another six months an' when he can he'll have to use a cane the rest of his life. Storekeeper, he wasn't even armed.'

The silent Whittier, the man named Jubal, said, 'Let's go', to his brothers and the three of them left the store.

Rufe wilted, was still leaning on the counter when Bert Freeman walked in grinning. As usual, he hadn't washed or shaved and his streaked grey hair was uncombed. He said, 'Good afternoon to you, Rufe. I just run into them Whittier boys. They give me a gold piece, five dollars' worth. I'd like to buy some tinned peaches, a tin of cookin' soda and some Mule Shoe.'

Rufe gazed steadily at the old man. 'You miserable son of a bitch,' he said without raising his voice. 'You told them Beulah didn't have a daughter, didn't you?'

'Well, there's nothin' to get high'n mighty about. She don't have a daughter. Never did have. I've known Beulah close to fifteen years. She don't have no kin of any kind. You want to get them things? I'll pay cash money.'

Rufe removed the elegant six-gun from the drawer, put it on the counter and said, 'Don't you ever step foot in this store again or I'll kill you on sight. *Git!*'

Freeman left, Rufe put the pistol back in the drawer and slammed it. He went to his cubbyhole office, found the bottle, swallowed twice, got rid of the bottle and sank down in the room's only chair.

He was still sitting there when someone came in out front. He heaved up out of the chair, went out front and stared. Beulah said, 'Well, least you could do is say hello.'

'Hello. Is she still out there?'

'Maria Elena? Of course she's still out there. Why shouldn't she be?'

Rufe went behind the counter before saying, 'There's three brothers named Whittier after her. Holser shot their pa durin' a robbery. Crippled him for life.'

Beulah was interested but unworried. 'It worked with them federal deputies. What're you worried about?'

'They had two dodgers with pictures on 'em. It was Maria Elena as plain as I'm standin' here.'

Beulah looked around, went to the bench and sat

down. 'How'd they have her picture?'

'Beulah, they know she's at Will Hobart's place an' this time they won't be fooled. Bert told them you never had a daughter.'

'I'll kill him!'

'You'll have to wait your turn,' Rufe said, and leaned down on the counter. 'She's got to be hid an' I'd guess those Whittiers'll turn things upside down. They knew she came here. They know folks have been protectin' her. These aren't fellers eager to get back where they come from.'

'Does Jim know?'

Rufe shook his head. 'I'll hunt him up directly.'

'Rufe, he left a couple of hours ago ridin' west. You want me to guess where he's goin'? I told you, he's sweet on her.'

Rufe groaned aloud. 'If the Whittiers don't over-take him an' he gets all the way out there they won't be far behind.'

Beulah arose. 'I got to get a horse; I'd never be able to walk out there in time. Rufe, are you comin'? He's a friend of yours.'

Rufe ignored her last statement. 'Where can you get a horse?"

Beulah shrugged. 'That old grey mule of Jim's can be rode. He don't rein an' he don't go out of a walk. Are you comin' with me? Like I said, you'n him been friends a long time.'

Rufe hauled up off the counter with a visible effort. The prospect of making that long ride again wasn't pleasant. He rarely rode. Even when he went down yonder to replenish his inventory he rode in Jim Elsworth's wagon. Also, he was still sore and achy from his ride last night.

Beulah interrupted his thoughts when she said, 'If I don't quit lockin' up the eatery what customers I got will stop comin' around. He's headin' into real trouble, Rufe. Goin' out there to visit Maria Elena, innocent as a child of what's fixin' to happen.'

'Go get the damned mule, Beulah. One more time lockin' up the store an' folks'll be goin' down to Angelina for supplies.'

After Beulah departed, Rufe returned to his cubbyhole, dug out the bottle, took down two more swallows and blew out a flammable breath. 'Son of a bitch,' he said aloud, '*women!*'

Beulah was only partly right about the freighter's old mule. He'd never been broke to ride; he was old, accustomed to whatever Jim required of him so he tolerated being ridden, but with a streak of Missouri in him, he chose his gait. All the drumming on his ribs with heels accomplished was that the mule's intransigence became more pronounced.

Rufe wanted to make good time, but had to set the gait of his horse to that of the Elsworth mule. As he rode slumped and exasperated he constantly scanned the countryside. He had no idea where the Whittiers might be except that they could be somewhere up ahead.

He had one reassuring thought: if the Whittiers reached the Hobart yard before he and Beulah were close, Will Hobart, still testy over the earlier intruders, wouldn't be any happier to see the next batch.

Beulah was curious and also talkative. Never in her life had she been accused of reticence. She asked more questions about the Whittiers than Rufe could answer. Eventually his replies were down to grunts.

About halfway they saw what appeared to be four

or five horsemen rounding up and driving a band of cattle. They were heading them in a north-westerly direction. Beulah got agitated until Rufe said there were no more than three Whittiers and the distant men were gathering and driving, not manhunting.

She calmed down. 'The Houstons. You know 'em?'

Rufe knew the Houstons only casually through the store. They ran cattle at the furthest north-westerly edge of Hell's Canyon and above the canyon where there were miles of grassland. The Houstons, four sons and their father who was a widower, didn't favour the settlement. When they went for supplies they took two wagons and went down as far as Angelina.

The distance and dust made identification impossible but Rufe knew of no other large-scale stockmen in the canyon. Also, the direction was right.

He was concentrating on the distant horsemen when Beulah made an audible gasp. She was sitting sideways with her right hand on the mule's rump.

Rufe looked back. There were riders behind them riding in an easy lope and strung out. Three of them.

Rufe sat forward. He hadn't exactly anticipated this and he'd been watching the land. What had undoubtedly tricked him was the number of rolling places where there were arroyos. From a distance, the land looked flat; dips, arroyos and shallow canyons were only visible when horsemen came in sight of them.

He said, 'Smarter'n I thought, Beulah. They likely figured someone would head for the Hobart place an' settled in an arroyo until we passed.'

Beulah said, 'It's not much farther, we can maybe outrun 'em.'

Rufe considered the aged Elsworth mule and showed Beulah a wintry smile as he said, 'I don't think so.'

The pursuing riders neither picked up their gait nor slackened it. They were confident of overtaking the people ahead and that bothered Rufe a little too.

He had figured the Whittier boys about right. They were not just *coyote* they were unrelenting, hard and confident.

Rufe estimated the distance and shook his head. Hobart's yard was a good long country mile ahead.

He said, 'Beulah, might as well stop, let 'em come up an' get this over with.'

Her reply was in character. 'I should've brought the shotgun.'

Where they drew rein was near a bosque of middle-aged oak trees, neither thick nor thin. Oaks were some of the slowest growing trees known to man.

The Whittiers dropped down to a steady walk, closed the distance without haste, stopped a couple of hundred feet from Rufe and Beulah and the eldest Whittier, the one named Evan, called, 'Mornin', folks. You're a fair distance from the settlement.'

Beulah's retort was neither friendly nor meant to be. 'We could say the same for you. Who'n hell are you anyway?'

Evan remained unruffled. 'Ask your friend. Were you goin' to the Hobart place?'

Beulah flared up again. 'None of your business, mister.'

Evan Whittier drew, cocked his six-gun and pointed it at Beulah. 'Ma'am, I asked a civil question.'

Rufe sought to head off something serious so he said, 'We're goin' to the Hobart place. Is that where you're headed?'

Evan holstered his six-gun, ignored Beulah and concentrated on Rufe. 'That's right, Storekeeper. That's where we're goin' an' I expect you know why.'

Somewhere up ahead someone fired a gun, twice, and after an interval fired it twice more.

8

Caught!

After the last echo had died Evan Whittier said, 'Mister Hobart must be fixin' to butcher,' and the middle Whittier drily said, 'He must be a damned poor shot.'

Evan gestured toward Rufe. 'You'n the old woman lead the way.'

Beulah's reaction could have been anticipated. 'Who're you callin' an old woman, you unwashed-lookin' whelp?'

Evan smiled, offered no response and nodded for Rufe to resume riding.

He and Beulah hadn't made good time since leaving Hellsville. They did not increase their gait now. The Whittiers trailed them from a distance of roughly fifty feet. Nothing was said until they had the Hobart yard and buildings in sight, then Evan casually said, 'Poor grazin' country.'

No one took that up. Where the canyon's high bluffs made a curve, thick stands of trees were visible where the cliff faces seemed to impede any upward route. There were trails but none of the five riders were interested. They had their full attention on the yard where three dogs raised hell and propped it up.

Rufe off-handedly said, 'Mind the black one, he bites.'

This comment elicited no response. When they entered the yard, Rufe watched the wide doorless front barn opening. Will Hobart had a knack of being in there.

He wasn't. They tied up at the barn's rack and Evan Whittier told Rufe to sing out, which Rufe did and got the immediate kind of response a man could give who had watched the riders enter his yard.

'Who's with you, Rufe, besides *her*?'

Evan called back, 'My name's Whittier. These gents are my brothers. Is the Messican woman in the house?'

Hobart called back. 'There's no Messican in here.'

'Who's in there with you, Mister Hobart?'

'Ask Beulah, it's her daughter.'

Evan's middle brother made a dour smile but said nothing. Clearly the eldest Whittier was spokesman.

Evan's voice remained calm. 'Mind if we come over an' talk?'

'I mind. What'd you say your name was?'

'Evan Whittier. These are my brothers, Jubal an' Herbert.'

'What do you want to talk about, Mister Whittier?'

Evan leaned on the tie rack studying the house. 'An outlaw named Holser shot our pa during a robbery south of here a ways. The storekeeper told us where Holser's buried. Marshal Alvarado from Angelina shot Holser an' he died. He wasn't alone when he robbed my pa's store. He had a Messican woman with him. Mister Hobart, you got her in the house.'

This time Will Hobart sounded sarcastic when he

replied, 'Beulah's daughter is here with me. She's a 'breed In'ian. There's just the two of us.'

Evan Whittier straightened up. 'We're comin' over, Mister Hobart.'

'Come ahead, you'll be sittin' ducks. I got some age on me but I don't miss up close. Come ahead.'

Rufe spoke to the burly Whittier. 'He'll shoot.'

Evan looked from the house to Rufe as he addressed his brothers. 'Herb, go over by them easterly sheds. Jubal, go out through the back of the barn. Stalk the house. Be careful.'

Before the men split up, Beulah addressed the eldest Whittier. 'You'll get yourselves hurt and there's a woman in there.'

Whittier fished in a pocket, brought forth the dodger, held it up for Beulah to see and had no reason to speak; Beulah's expression confirmed what he suspected. He put the poster away and jerked his head for his brothers to move.

They did. Will Hobart saw one enter the barn, the other one went toward the sheds and passed from sight. Hobart called to the muscled-up men. 'You make war here, mister, an' it'll end up like it did yestiddy when them two US marshals was here.'

Evan called back in a voice of confidence, 'They was young'n green, Mister Hobart.' Evan paused. 'We aren't goin' to shoot it out with you, we're goin' to burn your house down.'

Beulah started to speak. Evan Whittier caught her by the arm and spun her facing him. He held a double-edged boot knife to her chest. 'Not another word out of you. Understand, old woman?'

Rufe interceded. 'She understands.'

Beulah turned on Rufe, stiffly erect and glaring.

'Are you goin' to stand there an' let 'em burn my daughter?'

Rufe shook his head without replying.

Evan Whittier herded Rufe and Beulah into the barn where it was both cool and fragrant. He said, 'Walk into the granary. Leave your weapons outside. *Move!*'

As with many barns, the granary was built against both the front wall and the southerly back wall. It smelled of equal parts grain in piled sacks, and rats. When the door was closed the granary was dark.

Rufe sat on a sack of feed. Beulah hovered near the door. As with other granaries like this one there was a hasp. The custom was not to lock the door but to close it and drop a bolt through it where a lock was supposed to go.

Rufe tried the door. From the far side Evan Whittier said, 'Get comfortable, Storekeeper. Without an axe you won't get that door open.'

It was the truth; granary doors as well as walls were built to discourage any kind of intrusion, two-legged or four-legged.

Rufe returned to his grain-sack seat but Beulah groped and prowled, occasionally muttering to herself.

Rufe knew better than to test the east or south walls. He felt his way to the door again and examined it with both hands. Hinges were commonly put on the outside so the door would swing outward, but not always. If there had been hinges on the inside he would have found them. All he found was where bolts came through to secure outside hinges.

He felt each nut - called a 'burr' – and wasn't surprised that they had rusted and, as was commonplace during the rust process, the threads had fused. Nothing short of a twenty pound maul would break them loose. Granaries don't have mauls, they have sacks of feed.

Someone called from the house. The words were indistinguishable but the voice belonged to Will Hobart. Even if the granary prisoners could have understood the words they wouldn't help their plight.

What Hobart had called was something different from anything he'd said before. 'Mister Whittier? I'm willin' to talk.' The prisoners heard Whittier's response easily. It was given in the same confident voice as before. 'Not much to talk about, Mister Hobart. We come for the woman an' we won't leave without her.'

After a long pause Hobart called again. 'You come over to the house. Just you alone, an' we'll talk.'

This time the burly man's reply sounded almost amused. 'You think we come down in the last rain, Mister Hobart? We're not goin' to your house until it's ashes.'

Rufe leaned against the door which made it rattle. Evan Whittier growled, 'Set easy in there. Even a damned rat couldn't get through that door.'

Rufe continued to lean. He had been unable to make out much of what Will Hobart had said but he could catch an inference from Evan Whittier's answers.

During the exchange of calls, Beulah felt her way close and said, 'Never mind mouthy in the barn. Where are them other two?'

There was nothing wrong with the question except that it was unanswerable so Rufe pushed harder to

listen ignoring Beulah. She passed along the walls of
rough wood like a blind person, feeling her way with
both hands. She did that three times; she had nothing else to do except worry.

Someone whistled. Beulah hastened back where
Rufe was straining to hear. She didn't get to the door
until Rufe heard someone challenged from the barn
doorway.

'What do you want here?'

The reply was slow coming and when it eventually
came the man's voice was raspish. 'Who are you,
mister?'

The elder Whittier answered, but belatedly. 'Evan
Whittier. Who are you?'

His question wasn't answered. Instead, the rough-
voiced man said, 'You alone, Mister Whittier?'

'No. I got two brothers.'

'Have you now, an' where are they?'

Evan's temper showed in his reply. 'What are you
doin' here? Who are you?'

The other man's voice was easy to remember. He
said, 'My name's Ira Houston. These are my boys, Eb
an' Jim. I'll ask you again, what are you doin' here?'

'We want to talk to Will Hobart.'

Again the man with the raspish voice sounded
dour. 'When you want to talk to folks is it your
custom to lay siege?'

Evan had reason to resent this intrusion. He said,
'Mister, turn that horse. You'n your boys go back wherever you come from. This is none of your business.'

The sound of someone expectorating was audible
even through the granary door before the man on
horseback spoke again. 'Mister, don't no outlanders
come into our canyon an' give us orders.'

Someone cocked a gun. Evan Whittier's voice sounded slightly different when next he spoke. 'Put that gun up, mister. My brothers'll blow you apart. *Put it up!*'

Will Hobart called from the house, 'Ira, you're a sight for sore eyes.'

The mounted, older man with a cud in one cheek raised his eyes toward the house, leaned with both hands atop the horn and called back. 'We heard the signal shots, Will. We was drivin' back drifters. What're you up to?'

Hobart answered clearly. 'Those three want an In'ian girl in here with me. Beulah Bell's daughter.'

Again the mounted man's response was delayed. 'Why'd they want her . . . Beulah's daughter?'

'They want her for helpin' a feller named Holser rob their pa's store somewhere down south. Carter Alvarado shot her man down in Angelina. He died. They want her for helpin' him rob stores.'

In the moment of silence following Hobart's harangue, someone over by the log storehouse cocked a carbine. Ira Houston and his sons looked in that direction. The father expectorated a second time before calling loudly, 'You there behind the shed, come out an' put that gun on the ground.'

No one appeared. Evan Whittier sounded triumphant when he addressed the elder Houston again. 'Mister, turn tail an' keep on ridin' or the ma of your boys'll be cryin' her heart out tonight.'

Houston answered bluntly. 'My woman's been dead nine years.' He paused, gave a slight nod of the head, reined around and led the way with his sons out of the yard.

Evan Whittier called to Hobart again. 'You got ten

minutes to send the Messican woman out before the fire starts.'

There was no response from the house for a long time. Rufe's anxiety increased by the minute. Unless Will Hobart could be in two places at the same time one or the other of the younger Whittiers would set fire to the house.

Beulah swore and rattled the door with her fist. The only acknowledgment she got was a curt, 'Shut up in there or I'll burn the damned barn with you two in it. *Shut up!*'

Beulah obeyed their captor. She turned on Rufe. 'Are you goin' to stand there an' let 'em set fire to the . . .'

'No! I'm goin' to chew a hole in the door like a rat, grab that son of a bitch and eat him alive. Beulah, shut up!'

Her answer was in character. 'An' I always figured you'd be a good man to be in a fix with. I was wrong.'

Evan was in the process of yelling to his brothers when a bullet splintered wood in the front of the barn. It was accompanied by the sharp report of either a rifle or a carbine. Because rangemen did not carry rifles, the shooter had to have fired a saddle gun.

Evan jumped sideways, fell against the granary door and loudly swore. Beulah made one of her uncomplimentary remarks. 'Scairt the whey out of that big brave cowboy.'

Rufe felt rather than heard Evan pull up off the door. He also heard something else, a piece of steel hit the barn's earthen floor, and held his breath. The only loose-fitting length of steel he knew of was that old wagon bolt that held the door latch of the granary.

Two men were shouting. One was on the east side of the yard behind a log shed. The other shouter was Evan Whittier when he yelled back, 'I'm all right. The son of a bitch missed by a yard.'

Silence lingered until the hidden Whittier called reproachfully to his brother in the barn. 'Why'd you let 'em ride away?'

Evan didn't answer. He picked up his hat, knocked dust from it against his trouser leg and swore, not loudly but with feeling.

Rufe scarcely breathed. Evan Whittier was walking toward the rear barn opening. He evidently thought the shot had come from out there somewhere.

Rufe pushed very gently. The door yielded. Beulah was at his shoulder. 'We got no weapons. He'll shoot you, Rufe.'

It was another of Beulah Bell's remarks that could be ignored. Rufe had not a single doubt that what the elder Whittier had said about firing the barn with Rufe and Beulah inside it was true.

He eased the door open far enough to see his handgun lying in the dust where he'd dropped it about fifteen feet from the front barn opening.

He pushed a little more, enough to be able to peek past toward the rear of the barn.

Evan Whittier was standing to one side of the opening concentrating on scanning the country beyond and out back where there was no cover, not a single tree and, except for a tilted stack of meadow hay, there was nothing to interfere with the flat plain all the way to the furthest cliff face where a faintly discernible trail led upward.

Without warning a shot sounded from the west, somewhere among the gullies and arroyos out there, again in an area where, excepting a bosque of middle-aged oaks, there was no cover. The gunshot had not come from the northerly oaks, it had come from somewhere directly westward. There was nothing to be seen out there and the two younger dogs barked their heads off. The older black dog ducked under the porch. He was gun shy.

After the last echo, Will Hobart or someone who had the same kind of rough voice called from the house.

'You there on the west side of the well house, throw your weapons away or the next shot'll take your head off!'

Evan Whittier had whirled at the sound of the second shot. Rufe sucked slowly back and hoped for all he was worth the elder Whittier would not notice the granary door was open a foot.

Whittier seemed bewildered. He seemed about ready to hike up front when another voice called, 'You there in the barn, throw your guns out!'

Instead of obeying, Evan sprang to one side where he was protected by the log wall and whoever had called to him let fly a single gunshot and followed that with another shout. 'Throw 'em out or your wife'll be a widow. I said throw your guns out. *Now!*'

Evan neither disarmed himself nor moved from his protected place. He was staring toward the front barn opening. Rufe eased the granary door closed an inch at a time and when it was in place Beulah, for once in her life, lowered her voice. 'They got 'em surrounded.'

Rufe did not comment. There were three Houstons. Only two had shouted. But when another shout came he thought he knew where the third Houston was – inside the house.

Beulah spoke again. 'Tell the son of a bitch to do what they say.'

Rufe leaned to see if Evan was coming up through toward the front barn opening. During a period of silence he could not hear a sound.

Beulah said, 'You should've taken a chance an' jumped for your gun.'

Finally Rufe replied, 'Jump twenty feet? Even a rabbit can't jump that far an' he's holdin' a Colt in his right hand.'

'Well. . . .'

'Beulah, do me a favour. Shut up!'

The initiative had passed to Will Hobart's neighbours. Rufe was thankful they had been rounding up strays close by. What he might also have been thankful for if he had known it was that by a pre-arranged signal going back many years, Will Hobart and the Houstons had an agreement that if either were in serious trouble they would signal about it with two gunshots, a wait, then two more gunshots.

The invisible Houston west of the yard called again. 'You bastard, I can see you plain as day. Shed the gun right damned now!'

The Whittier on the west side of the log shed could reach the corner and duck around it in seconds. A wiser individual would have expected the invisible gunman to have his gun steady and aimed. He could pull the trigger in one second.

Whittier took down a deep breath, dug in his heels and jumped. The bullet caught him in mid air. He screamed, fell against the log wall and crumpled still screaming. It was an unnerving sound to those who heard it, but particularly to his brothers.

Evan started toward the front of the barn keeping as far to one side as he could. Rufe heard him coming. Beulah nudged him. He would have lashed out under different circumstances. He waited until the footfalls were abreast of the door then eased it open a fraction, saw the part of Whittier that was not obscured by the door, waited and when the burly man's entire back was to him, he slammed the door as far as it would go and made his run.

Evan Whittier had been distracted when the granary door struck other wood. He was turning when Rufe hit him. In weight and build they were evenly matched, but Whittier had a gun in his hand.

Rufe's momentum knocked Whittier backward. When they both went down they were head and shoulders in sunlight past the door.

Whittier swung his six-gun overhand. Rufe had Whittier in a two-handed grip. He leaned as far as he could but the gun barrel struck him a glancing blow. There was no pain, not then, that would come later.

Whittier pitched upwards. Rufe struck him below the left ear. Whittier briefly sagged then threw all his weight upward and sideways to dislodge his attacker.

Rufe concentrated on the fisted pistol. He used both hands to keep it away. The effort cost him every ounce of his strength.

Whittier bared his teeth and swung his left fist. For seconds Rufe had difficulty focusing his eyes. He hung on to the gun wrist as they struggled.

Whittier suddenly loosened all over. Beulah had grabbed a nearby double tree from a harness rack and swung it hard. She drew back for another blow but it was not needed. Blood showed through Whittier's hair.

9

'No, you don't.
Yes, I do!'

Two Whittiers were out of the fight. Evan Whittier
had a bloody scalp; pain would not come until he
regained consciousness.

Beulah brought an old lass rope which Rufe used
to lash the unconscious man's wrists behind his back
and his ankles. Beulah leaned on her weapon, watching. As Rufe was arising she said, 'That's one son of a
bitch that'll set things out.'

Hobart yelled from the house for the wounded
Whittier on the east side of the yard to come to the
house and get cared for.

The injured man neither made the effort nor
continued his outcries. From the house Hobart said,
'Dead.' There was no reason to doubt him.

Rufe went out back and identified himself, asked
for the sniper somewhere in the vicinity of the hay
stack to show himself.

That didn't happen. Evidently for the Houstons
who knew none of the strangers, until they knew
otherwise everyone in the yard was their enemy.

The wounded Whittier's outcries became groans,

not loud enough to cover the sound of a running horse.

Beulah did a thoughtless thing. She carried the harness tree when she walked out of the barn and continued to walk in plain sight all the way to the house where she disappeared inside.

Rufe remained in the barn, was still there when a harsh voice sang out, 'Will, I got the one in back of the shoein' shed. He's not dead, he's got a busted leg.'

Hobart recognized the voice and called back, 'Ira, there's one in the barn an' another one skulkin' somewhere.'

Rufe could whittle the odds a little and did. He called from inside the barn. 'It's Rufe, Will. I got the one in the barn.'

Hobart answered. 'I know. Beulah's told us. Where's the other son of a bitch?'

Rufe had no idea so the silence returned and lingered. All three dogs were cowering under the porch as silent as mice. Rufe lingered near the rear barn opening. He now knew where the older Houston was. What he didn't know was where his sons were but that minor mystery was abruptly resolved by two gunshots and a man yelling in a high voice.

'I give up.'

'Come out where I can see you – unarmed!'

Rufe placed the voices, the man who surrendered was close to the main house. He evidently walked out because one of the Houstons said, 'Walk toward the sound of my voice!'

There was another interlude of silence before the Houston named Eb spoke loudly. 'Lie down on your belly! Good; both hands out in front. *Do it, you son of a bitch!'*

Ten seconds passed before Eb Houston spoke again, in a lower voice this time. 'Stand up, face around an' give me your belt.'

'My pants'll fall down.'

'Give me the belt!'

Rufe risked leaving the barn. He could see the captor lashing a rumpled man's arms behind his back. Eb Houston used his six-gun as a prod heading his prisoner in the direction of the main house.

Rufe went back up through the barn and stopped when Evan Whittier groaned. Rufe toed him over on to his back. Whittier's face and head were bloody. He had to squint upwards.

Rufe leaned, caught hold in two places and hoisted Whittier to his feet and had to steady him or he would have collapsed. He said, 'It's over. We're goin' to the house . . . you understand me?'

Whittier groaned and feebly nodded his head. 'What'd you hit me with?'

Rufe didn't answer, he held Whittier with one hand. 'Walk; I can't carry you.'

They got as far as the front barn opening before Evan Whittier sagged. 'Can't make it,' he said without raising his head.

'You'll make it.'

'My head feels like it's comin' to pieces.'

Rufe tugged. 'One foot in front of the other. Let's go.'

This time they got midway before Whittier groaned and would have fallen if Rufe hadn't held him upright. Whittier said, 'Where're my brothers?'

'One's at the house with a hurt leg. The other one gave up.'

They covered another few feet before Evan raised his head. 'How'd you get out of the granary?'

'Don't talk, just walk.'

They had trouble with the three broad, wide steps leading up to the porch. Ira Houston and Will Hobart came out to help. They got the injured man as far as a chair on the porch where he sagged for the last time. They eased him into the chair.

Will Hobart disappeared into the house and reappeared with whiskey. Evan Whittier swallowed twice, pushed the bottle away and coughed. Immediately after coughing he groaned and fainted.

Will Hobart looked at Rufe. 'What'd she hit him with?'

His answer came from the doorway where Beulah was standing. 'With the first thing that come to hand. A double tree.'

Hobart scowled. 'You like to killed him.'

Beulah was not contrite. 'I'd have shot the son of a bitch if I could've.' Beulah stepped aside for Eb to herd his prisoner into the house. She made a caustic comment. 'Gettin' crowded, Will.'

Hobart did not respond. He followed the men inside.

Moments later the men on the porch heard Beulah berating the only Whittier who was uninjured. 'You damned idiot. You boys liked to have got yourselves killed for no reason.' She paused to call, 'Daughter, come out here.'

Maria Elena startled even the men who knew her. For one thing her upper lip protruded. For another thing she was heavily upholstered and had what could have been a knife scar over the bridge of her nose. Beulah faced Evan Whittier.

'This here is my daughter. Her pa was a full blood Dakota. Where's that Wanted dodger?'

'Jubal has it.'

'Get it. Will, untie his arms. Go get the dodger!'

Whittier went out where his brother's colour had improved but his eyes watered copiously. When he handed over the dodger, Jubal unfolded it, studied it and wagged his head. 'It's not the Messican woman, Evan. Come inside an' see for yourself.'

Evan made no move to arise from the chair. He looked up and said, 'I need a doctor, Jubal. I think my skull's cracked.'

Jubal held the dodger for Evan to look at. Evan pushed it away. Jubal repeated it. He said, 'Come look at her.'

Evan lowered his head, raised both hands to support it and muttered through his fingers, 'I don't give a damn. I got to find a doctor.'

Ira Houston was leaning against the porch railing. 'Nearest one's down at Angelina.'

Evan again spoke through his fingers. 'Get him up here. I can't ride that far.' He moved his hands and looked at Ira Houston. 'Send someone for him. I'll pay what he wants. Just send someone.'

Will Hobart and Ira Houston exchanged a look before Ira said, 'Herb can go. He needs to get his leg tended to. Will, you want to keep Evan here or want him taken to the settlement?'

Beulah interrupted from the doorway. 'Let the son of a bitch die.'

Ira Houston barely inclined his head. 'Most likely. Will. . . ?'

'I'll put him up, Ira. He don't look like he could stand a lot of movin'.'

Beulah snorted in the doorway. 'Animal gets a broken leg you shoot him,' she said, and returned to the parlour, considered the dour, silent men and jerked her head for Maria Elena to follow her to the kitchen.

Rufe sat on a bench opposite Jubal Whittier. 'How bad's your brother that got shot in the leg?'

Jubal looked and acted disgusted. 'The way he was writhin' an' cryin' a person would have thought his back was busted. Bullet went through his leg above the knee. It's tied off.' Jubal looked at the sweating, pale, wounded man. 'I've seen men hurt worse an' they never stopped singin'.'

Rufe went to the kitchen. Maria Elena avoided his gaze but Beulah didn't. 'Makin' that scar was hardest. We used some of Will's fast dryin' paint, sort of a clear varnish. It dried perfect. I expect it'll crack after a while.' Beulah saw the way Rufe was eyeing the younger woman and completed her explanation. 'Tore a flannel sheet, soaked it and folded it under her upper lip. She can't talk good.'

Rufe leaned in the doorway watching the women work at preparing a meal that he doubted anyone would eat. Jubal Whittier came up to say, 'We got to leave Evan here.' His expression was easily read. He was worried about his own fate.

Rufe pushed past without speaking, returned to the porch where Will Hobart and Ira Houston had moved further along the porch and were conversing in lowered tones. Will saw Rufe coming and said, 'That damned woman . . . did she have to hit him so hard?'

Rufe nodded. 'She had to.' He faced the elder Houston. 'Has Herb gone for the doctor?'

Houston nodded, considered Rufe for a moment before speaking. 'We was wonderin' what'll happen after those lads are fit to travel. Will they come back? Maybe with hired guns?'

Rufe had no answer. Up until this moment he hadn't thought of consequences and for that reason all he could do was shrug and say, 'I got no idea. It'll be up to the one named Evan, the feller Beulah hit over the head. Right now, lookin' at him I'd make a guess the sooner he can get away from here the better he'll like it. What he does afterwards, who knows?'

A solitary rider appeared in the middle distance. Will Hobart said, 'Now, who the hell,' and Rufe answered drily, 'Only person I know who rides a mule is Jim Elsworth.'

Hobart wasn't placated. 'What's he want? It's been a long time since I've had so many people around an' I don't like it.'

Rufe went to the barn. When the freighter entered the yard and saw the storekeeper he asked questions.

Rufe waited until Elsworth had led Estralita inside to be stalled and forked some feed, then began explaining.

Jim Elsworth pointed where Rufe was standing. 'That's blood,' he said.

'From the feller Beulah hit with a double tree.'

They were ready to leave the barn when Maria Elena appeared. Jim stopped in his tracks staring.

Rufe said, 'Beulah's idea; make her look like a knife-cut squaw.'

Someone called from the house. Rufe left Maria

Elena and Jim in the barn.

The uninjured Whittier man was eating in the kitchen with Beulah hovering. Across from him, Will Hobart ate, drank coffee and said, 'You're the one called Jubal?' and when Whittier nodded Hobart spoke again. 'You related to Jubal Anderson Early?'

Jubal stopped chewing. 'I been asked that fifty times. Until Pa told me who Jubal Anderson Early was I'd never heard of him. My folks was Unionists not Confederates.'

Hobart pushed his empty plate aside. 'I soldiered with Gen'ral Early when we marched on Washington. Scairt the hell out of Abe Lincoln.'

Because neither Jubal Whittier nor anyone else seemed interested Will Hobart let the subject die.

Jubal said, 'Herb'll get his leg patched up down in Angelina. We heard they got a good doctor down there.' He paused. 'Herb's tough. How many men do you know who'd make a long ride with a gunshot leg?'

No one spoke until Beulah glared and said, 'Drink your coffee.'

When Maria Elena and Jim Elsworth came inside, Jim looked shocked. The sight of bloodied Evan Whittier didn't ameliorate the shock. He went to Rufe and said, 'That one looks like hell. How bad's he shot?'

Beulah answered. 'He wasn't shot, I hit the son of a bitch with a double tree.'

Ira and his boys left. The day was spent; it would be dusk before they got home. Will Hobart went to the barn with them. For a cranky individual his expression of gratitude was genuine. Ira was swinging over leather when he said, 'Next time it might be me. You

take care, Will. If things fix to get out of hand, you
know the signal.'

Maria Elena and Beulah got Evan Whittier to a
bedroom that had no window and smelled musty.
When Hobart returned from seeing the Houstons
on their way he stood in the bedroom doorway
watching the women make Evan comfortable on the
bed. He offered advice. 'Get him a full glass of
whiskey.'

The women neither moved to obey nor showed
awareness of his presence.

Evan's hair was crusted. His head and shoulders
were covered with drying blood. Beulah stood back,
hands on hips and said, 'Daughter, get the shirt off
him. I'll get a pan of hot water.'

As Beulah left the bedroom she swept the man in
the doorway along with her.

Evan Whittier's eyes were swollen almost closed,
but they focused. He watched Maria Elena who
thought he was too ill to be conscious until he said,
'You was Holser's horse-holder, wasn't you?'

Beulah had drilled her in several Dakota words.
She wasn't sure which ones fitted this situation but
she looked straight at Whittier and said, '*Dina sica*.'

Whittier regarded her steadily through slitted eyes
when he said, 'What's no good?' and rattled off a
sentence she didn't understand. She fled to the
kitchen where Beulah listened before going to the
bedroom, looked at the injured man and singed his
sensibilities in Dakota before switching to English.

'You leave that girl alone or I'll finish what I
started in the barn.'

Evan would have looked bad even if he'd shaved.
The pain was there but somewhat less. He regarded

Beulah with no indication of being intimidated and spoke quietly.

'That's her. She was the only woman in the house. Someone doctored her up but that's her an' you know it.'

Beulah cocked her head slightly while regarding the bloody caricature of a rangeman. My man was Dakota.'

'But she—'

'*Shut your gawddamned mouth an' keep it shut!*'

Whittier obeyed, he felt too poorly to do otherwise.

Beulah spoke again. 'Mister, you keep goadin' me an' so help me I'll kill you. . . . She's my daughter, part Dakota not Messican. Get that through your damned, busted head. You understand what I'm sayin'? You make trouble for her an' I swear by Gawd I'll kill you!'

After Beulah departed, Evan Whittier closed his eyes. *She'd do it. That damned old witch would kill him and in his present condition there was nothing he could do to prevent it.*

The following afternoon, Doctor Harold Foster drove into the yard in a top buggy, left his animal at the barn tie rack and came to the house carrying a black satchel.

The house smelled of wood smoke which was tolerable, most houses smelled that way. But in the parlour where he met Hobart, Rufe, Jubal Whittier and Beulah Bell, the atmosphere was sour.

Jubal arose. Beulah told him to sit down. Rufe took the physician to the bedroom where he stopped stone still at sight of the man in the bed.

Rufe said, 'He got hit over the head,' and Doctor

Foster nodded. He'd heard this and much more from Herbert Whittier whom he'd patched up and left bedded down in Angelina.

He went to the bed, put his satchel aside, shed his coat and rolled up his sleeves as he said, 'A basin of hot water.'

After Rufe departed, the medicine man leaned to remove Evan's blood-stiff shirt. As he was doing this, Evan said, 'That old woman liked to killed me with a double tree.'

Doctor Foster leaned without saying a word. As he was straightening back he held up both hands. 'Can you see me do this?'

Evan could. The physician then asked Evan's full name and where he lived. The answers were given in a firm voice.

'How old are you?'

'Thirty-six.'

'Your father's name?'

'Micah Whittier.'

'Your mother's name?'

'Abigail Henderson Whittier. She died six years ago.'

'What are you doing here?'

This time Evan Whittier remained silent. Doctor Foster had heard from Herbert all he had to know concerning the reason the Whittiers were in Hell's Canyon.

Rufe brought a large basin with hot water in it. Behind him Beulah came into the room carrying clean cloths draped over one arm. Her gaze at Evan Whittier was bleak and unwavering.

It required two hours for Doctor Foster to do what could be done. As he was rolling down his sleeves he addressed the man in the bed. 'Mister, you have a skull thicker'n the skull of a Durham bull. By all rights you should have a concussion. If you're a prayin' man now would be a good time to give thanks.'

As the physician was shrugging into his coat he also said, 'Beulah'll take care of you. Don't try to stand up for a week.'

Doctor Foster went in search of Will Hobart and when he found him he said, 'Keep him quiet. Don't let him get up for a week. Two dollars, please.'

Will reddened. Beulah was standing in the kitchen doorway looking at him. Will cleared his throat, groped in a trouser pocket, drew forth a small roll of greenbacks held by a piece of string.

He handed over two dollars, stood in the doorway watching the doctor drive out of the yard and said, 'Two dollars, for Chris'sake. I've worked a week for that much money.'

Beulah was looking at crestfallen Jubal Whittier when she said, 'He'll pay you back. If he don't die first.'

That last sentence brought Jubal to his feet. Beulah made a small humourless smile. 'Go see the son of a bitch if you want. Come back with two dollars for Mister Hobart.'

Jim Elsworth was at the barn feeding Estralita when Rufe walked in. Jim said, 'You look like hell. Don't old Hobart have a razor you could borrow?'

Rufe grinned. It was a pleasant change to be insulted by a friend. 'Doc Foster said Whittier'll be down for a week.'

'Hobart will like that.'

'Jim . . . Maria Elena's goin' to stay here to look after Whittier.'

'Why can't Beulah do it?'

'Because she'd kill him, I expect.'

'That means I got to ride out this far every day or two.'

'No, it don't.'

'Yes, it does!'

10

The End – Maybe

As the days passed, Will Hobart got crankier. Maria Elena handled it well but on the fourth day when Beulah rode out on Estralita and Will met her at the door with a black scowl she only hesitated for a moment before putting a hand on his chest and pushing.

Inside, Beulah was shocked. The parlour was immaculate, furniture had been rubbed to a shine and there were wild flowers in a pitcher on the mantle.

Maria Elena appeared. Her disguise was gone. She smiled at Beulah. 'Come to see the patient?'

Hobart remained down at the barn where he could be alone with animals.

Evan Whittier had been washed, shaved and had his bandaged head on a clean pillow. He regarded the cause of his injury sombrely.

Beulah pushed a chair around, sat and leaned forward. 'If you give my daughter any meanness I'll cut your damned throat. Where are your brothers?'

'Gone. Jubal went down to Angelina to hire a rig to take Herb home.'

'Are they comin' back?'

117

'I told Jubal to tell Herb for the both of 'em to stay home, that I'd be along directly.'

Beulah did not look appeased. 'An' you're goin' to tell me they won't be back?'

'They won't.'

Beulah studied the freshly shaved face and leaned back in the chair. 'It took a cracked skull for you to get some sense. Your brother that got shot in the leg, maybe he'll get smart too. That leaves Jubal. He didn't impress me as a feller who wouldn't carry a grudge.'

Evan was annoyed. 'I told you they won't come back an' neither will I. You can believe it or not.'

Maria Elena leaned close to examine the bandage, straightened back as she said, 'It needs changing again.'

To Beulah the bandage looked fine. She arose. 'I want to talk to old sore tail.'

She reached the barn before a dog barked, stopped and looked westerly. Jim Elsworth was out a half-mile on his twenty-year-old, docile, grey horse-mule.

Hobart was wide-legged in the middle of the barn glaring past Beulah. 'Who the hell is that?' he growled.

She stepped in out of sunlight as she answered. 'Jim Elsworth. He's got a freighter camp some ways behind Rufe Malone's store.'

'What's he want here? I got no use for trespassers.'

Beulah considered Hobart whose expression was as pinched as though he'd been eating sour apples. She said, 'He's not comin' to see you, Will.'

Hobart faced Beulah. 'Whittier?'

'No, you blind old goat. Maria Elena.'

Hobart's hostile expression didn't change as he resumed his study of the approaching mule-man. 'Beulah, the girl needs a proper home.'

Beulah's eyes widened. 'Here?'

'She's a fine cook. Makes the best coffee I ever tasted.'

Beulah had colour rising in her face as she stared at Hobart. 'You want a housekeeper, hire one.'

'I thought on it. Room, board and ten dollars a month.'

'Are you talkin' about hirin' on Maria Elena for your housekeeper?'

Hobart had no difficulty picking up on the growing antagonism in Beulah's voice and became defensive. 'She needs a—'

'She don't need nothin' you have, Will Hobart! She's goin' back with me!'

When Jim Elsworth rode into the yard Beulah halted him with both hands on her hips. 'What do you want!' she snarled.

Elsworth was less surprised to find Beulah at the Hobart place than he was at her high colour and fierce stare. He drew rein about the time Will Hobart came out of the barn and said waspishly, 'Get you'n that damned mule out of my yard!'

Jim looked from one of them to the other, leaned and swung from the saddle. Will Hobart started toward him. Elsworth braced himself.

Beulah caught Hobart by the arms and swung him. He saw the fist coming and twisted to avoid it.

Jim Elsworth didn't move.

Hobart wrenched free and swore at Beulah.

Whatever Elsworth had ridden into didn't include swearing at women. He dropped his reins and started toward Hobart. Beulah blocked him.

'Stay out of this!' she exclaimed, and faced Hobart. 'Get out of my way.'

Hobart didn't move until Beulah started past then he got in front of her. Jim saw what was coming and this time when he started for Hobart, Beulah's back was to him.

'Hobart,' Jim said, 'you hit her an' I'll break your gawddamned neck!'

Hobart seemed frozen in place. His holstered Colt was on a peg on the wall in his bedroom. Jim Elsworth rarely wore a gun. For most altercations he didn't need one.

Beulah broke the standoff. 'Jim, you keep him here.'

Beulah went toward the house. She was at the steps when Maria Elena appeared in the doorway smiling at Beulah. Her smile winked out when Beulah said, 'Get your things. You're goin' back with me.'

Maria Elena looked past, out where Will Hobart and Jim Elsworth were standing. She returned her attention to Beulah when she spoke.

'He isn't ready yet. He can stand but he's weak. I can't leave him for another few days.'

Beulah's anger diminished. She considered Maria Elena. 'Is he well enough to come with us to the settlement?'

Maria Elena shook her head. 'Not for another few days, Beulah.'

Beulah stood at the lowest step when she said, 'Day after tomorrow I'll come for you both in my buggy. Maria Elena, it bothers me you bein' out here with that old boar.'

Jim Elsworth left Will Hobart by the barn, went as far as the steps and looked up. 'Are you all right?' he asked. 'Mister Hobart bother you?'

Maria Elena's gaze narrowed slightly on the freighter. 'No one's bothered me, Jim. Mister Whittier's doing well but he'll need watching for a few more days.'

Beulah relaxed, looked at Elsworth and wagged her head. 'You reason with her, Jim. I'm goin' back.'

Will Hobart hadn't moved. As Beulah came near, he said, 'What's wrong with you? I'm not Bert Freeman. She's as safe with me as she'd be with you.'

Beulah still felt hostile. 'You're a man, aren't you?' she exclaimed and entered the barn.

Hobart followed her. 'Beulah, I'd be glad to have that feller off my place. I'll bring him to the settlement in my wagon when Maria Elena figures he's well enough.'

Beulah looked steadily at Hobart. 'Three days, Will, not four days or five.' She rode out of the yard without looking at any of them.

Hobart went to the porch, tugged his hat low, watched Beulah grow small in the distance, ignored Jim and looked at Maria Elena.

'What in the hell's got into her?'

Elsworth answered before Maria Elena could. 'She's got it fixed in her head Maria Elena is her daughter.'

Hobart said, 'I'm hungry,' and followed Maria Elena into the house leaving Jim Elsworth to follow or not as he chose. He followed.

He felt uncomfortable even when Hobart set up the whiskey bottle and handed him a small glass. Without any way of Jim knowing it, the older man had just made a gesture of acceptance.

Evan Whittier's headache was gone. So many days in bed left him as weak as a kitten. He was polite to Will Hobart. With the passing of time they visited. They had a common ground, Will Hobart ran cattle and Evan Whittier had worked for cattlemen for a number of years.

It seemed to Maria Elena that Will Hobart looked forward to their visits; he'd no sooner finished supper than he would head for Whittier's room. They shared whiskey which heightened Whittier's colour, the earlier reserve faded. Maria Elena even heard them laugh a few times.

It was the older man who in his gruff way encouraged Whittier to walk. They moved through the house side by side. Evan Whittier was in his prime, he always had been a strong, active individual.

Maria Elena watched the morning Hobart took Whittier outside, across the yard to the barn. Whittier had no difficulty. Maria Elena sighed. She was no longer needed.

Beulah did not arrive on the third day. She drove into the yard on the fourth day, met Will Hobart at the barn and asked if Maria Elena was ready to leave. Hobart leaned on a three-tined hay fork as he was gazing past at the top buggy. 'It'll be a tight fit, Beulah. Your rig was made for two an' he's a pretty big feller.'

Beulah's retort was typical. 'We'll manage. Is she ready?'

Hobart nodded. 'She is. How about him?'

'He should be.'

'I expect so, except that no one's told him he's goin' to be moved to the settlement.'

Beulah spoke over her shoulder as she started for the house. 'I'll tell him.'

Hobart went back to his chores. Things weren't going to be the same. He had never encouraged familiarity and because of that he had been left alone.

He heard them coming, Maria Elena carrying a small bundle and the man beside her carrying nothing, but his shellbelt and holstered Colt were buckled into place. The bandage he wore was small enough not to interfere with his hat.

He looked presentable, pale and shy a few pounds, but Maria Elena had brushed his hat, had washed his clothes and had shaved him.

Where they stopped with Hobart leaning on the hay fork, Evan Whittier held out a closed fist. Hobart did not raise a hand to meet it. He said, 'What you got?'

'Fifteen dollars in gold for puttin' me up.'

Hobart looked steadily at the younger man. 'This isn't no hotel, boy. Folks don't take money for doin' what you do for 'em.'

Evan almost smiled. 'It's not for you, it's for dog food,' he said, and dropped the coins. Hobart watched as they got into the buggy and sure enough with Whittier between the women a person couldn't have got a cigarette paper between any of them.

Beulah unlooped the lines, looked out and said, 'See you at the settlement, Mister Hobart.'

He nodded, watched them leave the yard and when his dogs came over he stooped, picked up the money and said, 'You fellers are goin' to live high for a spell,' and went back to finish his chores.

There was very little conversation on the drive

back. For one thing Maria Elena could not antici-
pate her future. For another thing Evan Whittier
tried to squeeze enough so that the women weren't
crowded against the sideboards and wasn't very
successful.

Not until they had the settlement's small clutch of
buildings in sight did Beulah speak.

'I'd put you up, Mister Whittier, but I don't have
the room. Rufe Malone's got room at the store.'

She did not say whether she'd spoken to Rufe
about this and Whittier did not ask.

Maria Elena knew Beulah had a top buggy which
she kept in a shed with the shafts off the ground on
two small kegs. She also knew Beulah didn't own a
horse, but that was resolved when they drew up
behind the eatery and Beulah climbed down, made a
loud sigh of relief and let Evan Whittier help her
remove the harness and back the rig into its shed,
when an unwashed individual appeared grinning
like a tame ape.

Bert Freeman said, 'I told you that mare's as gentle
as a dog, Beulah.'

The older woman's reply was brusque. 'Come
inside, we'll eat.'

She led the way. Bert Freeman was the last through
the door and the first one to sit at the counter.
Beulah eyed him.

'I said one meal for use of the horse. You still owe
me for other meals, Bert.'

Freeman scratched beard stubble while looking
warmly at Beulah Bell. He said, 'How'd your girl get
that red place on her cheek?'

'Ask her,' Beulah replied, and went into her cooking area. Freeman didn't ask; Maria Elena explained

before he could. 'I peeled my cheek where it had some kind of paint on it.'

Evan Whittier regarded Maria Elena. 'It's no secret, is it?'

Maria Elena avoided facing the burly man without speaking. Beulah called from her kitchen. 'You was out there with her long enough to know, Mister Whittier.' Beulah appeared in the kitchen doorway. 'You got somethin' in mind, like takin' her down to Angelina to the law?'

Evan Whittier considered the older woman's iron-set jaw and unwavering stare. 'It wasn't hard to figure, ma'am. We was together for a spell.' Whittier paused. 'I come here to settle with the feller who shot my pa. He's out yonder. She held their horses. Far as I know she didn't have a gun. Missus Bell, when a man's bedridden he's got nothin' to do but ponder. She looked after me like a sister. I burnt that dodger in the stove out yonder. I'll tell you somethin': I was raised with the Dakotas. She'd never fool anyone who was. I owe you for hittin' me with that double tree, but that's another thing a bedridden man thinks about. You didn't have to hit me that hard but if you hadn't. . . . No ma'am, as far as I'm concerned she's your 'breed daughter. I got no idea what become of the other one, the one that held the horses.'

Beulah leaned in the kitchen doorway considering Evan Whittier. 'What about your brothers?'

The burly man shrugged. 'What about them? When I say she wasn't the Messican woman that'll end it.'

Bert Freeman squirmed on his seat. 'You goin' to feed us, or what? I wouldn't ride that horse to the settlement for just anyone.'

Beulah disappeared behind the old army blanket that separated her cooking area from the counter.

Bert Freeman shifted slightly on the bench until he and Maria Elena touched. He leaned to speak to Whittier, still grinning like a tame ape. 'That was quite a squabble,' he said. 'Will Hobart'll be a week gettin' back to normal.'

The discussion ended when a tall, lean stranger came in, looked around, went to the far end of the counter, sat down and thumbed back his hat.

Maria Elena left the bench to go behind the counter and ask the stranger for his order. He looked up from unsmiling eyes when he answered. 'Anything you got that's hot, with coffee.'

After Maria Elena went to the kitchen Bert Freeman leaned and addressed the stranger. 'You a cattle buyer, mister?'

The lean, unsmiling man regarded Freeman for a moment before replying, then all he said was, 'No,' and faced away from Freeman.

The food arrived. The stranger's platter arrived a little later. The atmosphere in the eatery became guarded.

Bert Freeman finished first, as with many bachelor loners he never turned down a woman-cooked meal. As he arose to thank Beulah, he said he'd ride the horse he'd loaned her and head for home.

No one missed Bert Freeman. Some years down the road when he died they still wouldn't miss him.

Beulah appeared in her kitchen doorway regarding the lanky man. He looked back. The others at the counter could sense the clash of wills.

Beulah addressed the lean, hawk-faced stranger. 'Are you passin' along or have you got kin here?'

The lean, tall man considered dowdy Beulah with an uncompromising gaze. 'I'm lookin' for a man named Rufus Malone. His store's closed up an' locked. Do you know him?'

Beulah snorted. 'Mister, in Hellsville everybody knows everyone else. I know him. Try the freighter camp easterly a ways. He might be out there.'

The stranger nodded, went back to his meal, ignored the older woman leaning in the doorway and the other diners and when he had finished eating he arose, put several coins beside the empty platter and walked out into the poorly defined roadway.

Beulah said, 'Lawman. I can smell 'em.'

Maria Elena cleared the counter and remained in the kitchen. Evan Whittier said he'd go out yonder and see if the storekeeper was out there. After he left, Beulah and Maria Elena cleaned up the kitchen. The younger woman was clearly anxious. She told Beulah if that stranger was a lawman he was probably after her and Beulah answered in character. 'If he is when he leaves the canyon he'll be a lot wiser an' sorrier a man than he is now.'

They had finished in the kitchen, took two cups of coffee out to the counter and were sitting there like a pair of worried crows on a fence when Will Hobart walked in. Beulah started to arise. Hobart said, 'Set. I didn't come to eat. Where's Whittier?'

Beulah told the stockman pretty much the same thing she'd told the stranger and after Hobart left, Beulah looked at Maria Elena smiling.

'If that stranger's here for trouble I got a feelin' he's goin' to walk into about all he can handle.' She considered Maria Elena. 'Would you like to walk out where your friend is buried? Say a prayer for him? I'm not much of a prayin' person but it can't hurt an' it's a fine day.'

Maria Elena was willing. It did not occur to her that the cemetery was far enough northward to provide a perfect view of most of the settlement and a particularly good view of Jim Elsworth's camp.

The grave was still mounded and would remain so until next summer after winter rains and snow had settled it.

There was a headboard, which surprised Maria Elena. It simply noted Wayne Holser's name and date of death. No date of birth, no little prayer which was the custom.

Maria Elena and Beulah Bell picked some wild flowers for the grave, and while Maria Elena was kneeling, head lowered, Beulah remained upright looking intently in the direction of the freighter camp.

There was no sign of Jim Elsworth, Rufe Malone or the stranger, but Jim's mules were out a ways grazing off seed heads the way horses and mules did when they were well enough fed to be choosy.

11

Another One – a Stranger

Rufe and Jim Elsworth left early to hunt in the high-lands. Usually game abounded. They tramped the noisy timbered country until close to noon. At least that's what the sun said; it was close to being at its daytime meridian. Neither man carried a watch. In fact, Jim did not own one. Rufe's watch had run down long ago. It was in a drawer in his living-quarters at the store.

They rested near one of the busy little creeks that fed the watercourse in the canyon.

It was a convenient place to rest. With their backs to a punky ancient deadfall, guns leaned aside, Jim startled his companion. 'I never been married. Have you?'

Rufe shook his head. 'Never wanted it to get in the way of other things.' He turned his head. 'Are you thinkin' about it?'

'Even with that red place on her cheek she's beautiful.'

Rufe could have agreed about that and except for Maria Elena having been the cause of all his recent

129

difficulties he would have. Instead he said, 'You mention it to her?'

'No. That's why I rode out to Will Hobart's place the last time and rode right into a fight between Will and Beulah.' Jim briefly ruminated before speaking again. 'Beulah's got the disposition of a bitch wolf.'

Again Rufe could have agreed, but instead he said, 'She's had a hard row to hoe; she wanted kids. Maria Elena come along. . . .'

'Hell, Rufe, she's worse than a sow bear with a cub.'

Rufe finally agreed. 'That's her nature. Jim?'

'What?'

'Don't move, just look up, a big tom turkey is settin' on a limb eyein' the creek.'

Jim didn't move, not until the turkey looked away, then in one swift, smooth movement he raised the gun and fired.

That was all they had to take back with them and it was a long walk; the most difficult part of which was descending into the canyon by way of a game trail peppered with boulders and wiry underbrush.

They got back about sunset and headed for the eatery to get Beulah to clean and pluck the turkey, which Jim placed atop the counter. When Beulah appeared from her cooking area, he said, 'Half is yours if you'll dress it.'

Beulah ignored the bird. 'Jim, there's a lawman lookin' for Rufe. I told him he might be at your camp an' haven't seen him since.'

Rufe sighed as he arose and lightly tapped the freighter's shoulder. After he left to open the store, Beulah addressed Jim Elsworth. 'What's the sense of ownin' a store if he goes traipsin' off turkey hunting?' She fingered the bird, held out its beard and would have said it was old and would be tough if Jim hadn't made his offer of a trade again.

'Half is yours for dressin' him.'

Maria Elena came in. Both Beulah and Jim looked at her, each with a different expression. She smiled at Jim, went to stand beside him when she addressed the older woman. 'He talked to Everett Merrit and Toby Johnson. Toby told me he said he had business with Mister Malone.'

Beulah lifted the bird, ignored Elsworth and jerked her head. After she and Maria Elena passed from sight Jim reluctantly arose. He had intended buying a meal.

Rufe was saved the indignation of shoppers when he unlocked the store. It was close enough to supper-time for customers to be at home.

He pulled up the bench and was in the act of light-ing the overhead lamp when a lanky travel-worn-looking stranger walked in. Rufe would have climbed down, but the tall man said, 'Finish lightin' it. I can wait another few minutes more. I been waitin' all day.'

When Rufe climbed down and put the bench aside, the lanky man said, 'You'll be Rufus Hamilton Malone?'

For several seconds Rufe said nothing. This was the first time he'd heard anyone use his middle name in years. He nodded.

'Mister Malone, my name is Andrew Wyeth. I work for the Pinkerton Detective Agency. You've heard of us?'

Again Rufe nodded. The lanky man could have passed for almost anything from a rangeman to a blacksmith, anything but a Pinkerton detective.

Rufe settled against the shelves at his back and crossed his arms. 'I did somethin' wrong, Mister Wyeth?'

Wyeth didn't answer until he found the bench and sat on it. 'I got a couple of questions if you don't mind? Did you ever hear of a man named Boston Corbett?' At Rufe's blank expression, Andrew Wyeth added more. 'The feller who assassinated President Lincoln was named John Booth. John Wilkes Booth.'

Rufe knew this much. When the president had been shot in Washington at Ford's Theater it would have been impossible not to know the details. For a year after the assassination every newspaper in the country had related the story.

Andrew Wyeth continued. 'They cornered the assassin, Booth, in a barn. When it was set afire to flush him, he ran out; couldn't run very good, he hurt his leg escaping from the theatre. A soldier shot him. A sergeant named Boston Corbett.'

Rufe remembered nothing except that act of assassination and the longer the Pinkerton man talked the more bewildered Rufe felt.

'Mister Malone, the feller Sergeant Corbett shot was in bad shape what with the fire an' all. But he had a busted leg and his brother identified the remains as being John Booth.'

Rufe finally interrupted. 'Mister, Hell's Canyon is about as far from the national capital as a man can get. I read and reread about the assassination. I expect everyone did. It was some years ago. The last I read they had the feller who shot the president.'

Wyeth fished forth a cheroot as he said, 'You mind?'

Rufe didn't mind. On rare occasions he had seen cigars like that. They were rare west of the Big River because they were expensive.

He watched the Pinkerton man light up and trickle smoke. He hadn't eaten since morning, had been hungry at Beulah's place but right now he felt no hunger at all.

'Mister Malone, the Pinkerton Agency's been hired to find John Booth.'

'You said he was dead.'

'I said Sergeant Corbett swore he shot him. Have you ever holed up in cold weather in a barn?'

'A few times. What's that got to do—'

'Mister Malone, there was a crippled Secesh soldier living in the loft of the barn. The man who owned the farm was a Confederate sympathizer during the war. He knew that Secesh was in his loft. He told us that much. He never did admit he was a sympathizer.'

Rufe stepped to the counter and leaned on it. 'Are you goin' to say that soldier shot the wrong man?'

'That's close, Mister Malone. The crippled Rebel had been shot in the hip. He didn't have a broken leg.'

'Sergeant Corbett . . . was it dark, Mister Wyeth?'

The lanky man nodded as he trickled smoke. 'Sergeant Corbett took it hard that he'd shot the wrong man.'

Rufe said, 'I can understand that. Mister Wyeth, why are you here?'

Wyeth crossed his legs. His gaze never left Rufe's face. 'It's a long story, Mister Malone. I'm here because we tracked the other man in the barn. A Maryland physician named Samuel Mudd set Booth's

broken leg. His description of Booth didn't fit the
man Sergeant Corbett shot.'

Wyeth tipped ash into a nearby sand box, considered the lighted end of his cigar and continued
speaking. 'We've been years on Booth's trail.'
Something close to an ironic smile showed on
Wyeth's face as he said, 'You'd be surprised how
many former Rebels with healed broken legs are
around. We investigated every one. Some of them
came West. It's taken years to eliminate men we
didn't want.'

Wyeth put out his cigar, uncrossed his legs and
leaned forward. 'There's six left out of hundreds.
Three we found and couldn't make the connection,
but every one of them was capable. Old Confederates
don't give up.' Wyeth arose facing Rufe. 'We tracked
some to the point where they disappeared. One we
tracked to a place near an Indian reservation going
by the name of William Small. He could have been
Booth. He had a limp; in other ways he fitted the
description.'

'You caught him?' Rufe asked.

Wyeth shook his head. 'He shot himself when he
was drunk. I'm not convinced he wasn't John Booth,
but there's still the other one. . . . Mister Malone, do
you know Doctor Foster down in Angelina?'

'I know him,' Rufe replied and stiffened. 'Not
him!'

'No. But when he first came here he worked on a
man whose leg had been broken years earlier and
who, according to Doctor Foster, was in constant pain.
He gave the man laudanum. That would stop the pain.
Doctor Foster described the man to me and said he
lived in Hell's Canyon. Mister Malone, Doctor Foster

said it was so long ago he didn't remember the man's name, only that he lived in Hell's Canyon.'

Rufe took down a breath and silently expelled it as the Pinkerton man said, 'You owning a store up here would probably know everyone.'

Rufe shifted position on the counter. As he did this the lanky man said, 'I know how you feel. Other folks have reacted the same way . . . I need your help to hunt down this last one.'

Rufe looked up. 'The only man I know who limps is a feller named Josh Henley. He told me he got charged an' run down by a cow buffalo with a calf. He was a hunter years back.'

'Which leg, Mister Malone?'

Rufe had to think. He couldn't remember which was the lame leg. He said, 'Damned if I know. He don't come to the store often.'

'Where does he live?'

'In a cobbled-together shack north of here about a mile.' Rufe wagged his head. 'He's quiet, minds his own business. Pot hunts an' sells meat around here an' down in Angelina.' Rufe remembered something. 'He has a buffler skull nailed over his door.'

Andrew Wyeth smiled for the first time. 'I'll buy you a drink,' he said and Rufe's answer was simple.

'There's no saloon in Hellsville.'

Wyeth considered before speaking again. 'There's a reward, Mister Malone. I'll go look up Josh Henley.'

Rufe continued to lean after the Pinkerton man's departure. He had been tired and hungry before Wyeth appeared. He still felt tired, more so in fact, but not hungry.

He took down the lamp, blew down the mantle, left it sitting on the counter and went out into the night heading for the mule-man's camp.

Jim Elsworth had already heard there was another stranger in the canyon but that was all he knew, so as he listened to Rufe his expression of incredulity deepened. 'That killin' was years back.'

Rufe's retort was from experience. 'The gov'ment never gives up. I told him old Josh Henley was the only man I knew who had a limp.'

Elsworth's incredulity deepened. 'Josh Henley, for Gawd's sake? I don't believe it. I've known him ever since I come into the canyon. Sure he limps, but I'll bet my mules he never assassinated anybody, not even In'ians.'

Rufe was sitting on an upturned little keg. He stood up. 'Somethin' about people, Jim; a man thinks he knows 'em then it'll turn out he really don't.'

That bit of philosophy was lost on the freighter. 'I know for a fact he's never been east of the big river. We've sat and talked lots of times. Old Josh was born in Messico an' spent all his life scrapin' by first as an army scout then as a teamster an' a buffler hunter.'

Rufe smiled. 'You don't have to convince me. Do you remember which leg he limps on?'

Jim didn't hesitate. 'The left one. Maybe I'd ought to go up there an' warn him.'

Rufe considered his old friend. 'Jim, between the two of us doin' what we figured was right is what got us into more trouble'n a man can expect if he lives to a hundred. Leave it to Josh an' the Pinkerton man.'

Rufe finally got to bed. He had meant what he had said to Elsworth; their good intentions had landed them in enough hot water to last a lifetime.

He didn't unlock the store until the sun was well

up and climbing. His first customer was Maria Elena. Beulah had sent her for a tin of baking powder.

After Rufe put the tin on the counter and brushed the coins in payment into his cash drawer, Maria Elena lingered.

He asked if there was something else and she smiled slightly without meeting his gaze. 'Have you known Jim a long time?'

Rufe sensed Maria Elena's interest before he said, 'Since he first come here with supplies for the store. He's honest, hard-workin' an' decent.'

Maria Elena still did not look up. 'He's courting me,' she said quietly, and Rufe could have said she hadn't said anything he hadn't already known. Instead he said, 'You could do a whole lot worse.'

She finally looked up. 'Freighters live in their wagons don't they?'

He nodded, 'Some of 'em do. They go where they're needed. It's kind of a nomad's way of life.'

'I want a home. Something of my own to come back to. A place where I can plant a garden, have flowers. I've never had a real home.'

Rufe had no answer for that fundamental difference between Jim Elsworth and Maria Elena. She thanked him and left. His next customer of the day was a prune-faced widow woman named Springer, old as dirt with little weasel eyes and an acerbic disposition. She said, 'I just saw Beulah's girl leave the store.'

From experience with the old woman, Rufe understood perfectly what she was aiming at and refused to be drawn into gossiping. 'Beulah ran out of baking soda,' he said and changed the subject. 'Wasn't your man a buffler hunter?'

The wizened widow nodded. 'An' after they was about gone he went to work haulin' their bones for a feller who ground them up an' sent 'em back East.'

'Do you know Josh Henley?'

The old woman put an irritable look on Rufe. 'Everybody knows Josh. Everybody in the canyon knows everyone else. My husband an' Josh Henley partnered for years until the bufflers was about gone.'

'Did he ever say much about Josh?'

The old woman's bright, intent eyes fixed on the storekeeper. 'Folks as asks questions got somethin' in mind,' she said. 'He told me him'n Josh hunted together for six years, except for once when they was young Josh left an' didn't return for half a year.'

After the old woman departed with her meagre purchases, Rufe went out front and stood in sunlight gazing northward. The old woman's last remark stuck in his mind. She had said Josh had once told her husband he didn't never want to go east of the Missouri again.

It didn't have to mean much although after his visit with the Pinkerton man it could be significant. The only way he could imagine to settle the question was for the old woman to remember what year Josh Henley had gone East and he had no faith in her ability to remember anything that had happened so long ago.

The following morning while Rufe was making the list of supplies that needed replenishing, Andrew Wyeth walked in, in his purposeful panther-like way of moving. Nodded and wasted no time.

'The wrong leg,' he said, before either of them had made the customary new day greeting.

Rufe put down his stub of a pencil, straightened up and said, 'How long was you up there?'

'We had supper,' Wyeth grimaced. 'In my line of work a man's got to sacrifice. Did you ever eat fried mush that smelled sour?'

Rufe grinned. 'I expect when you got to deal with folks like old Josh you got to make allowances.'

Wyeth nodded in agreement, considered the stocked shelves, returned his gaze to Rufe and said, 'You know, the last few years I've wondered what it'd be like to own a place like this where a man can stay indoors during hot weather and fire up a stove when snow flies.'

Rufe's little smile lingered when he replied, 'Them's the good parts. The bad parts is gettin' bawled out when you don't have what some mean old widow woman wants when she walks in. Or keep tabs for six months figurin' you'll never get paid. I've got a customer who ran a bill for about a year. He come in some time back an' paid some of it with gold.'

'Nuggets?'

'No. Gold eagles.'

'Why don't you just cut him off?'

'Because the old bastard'd starve durin' a bad winter. He don't really belong. He's a poor hunter, don't raise vegetables to be stored up, lives in a spur canyon like a damned hermit.'

Wyeth said, 'What's his name?'

'Bert Freeman. He's not exactly crazy, but I'd guess him to be borderline. Grins all the time. Keeps an old horse danged near as old as he is, acts like everything's a joke.'

Until Wyeth asked his next question Rufe had no

idea that Wyeth's entire existence was based on one thing: finding his man.

Wyeth said, 'Does he limp?'

Rufe hung fire before answering then shook his head and pithily said, 'Mister, I'm glad you're not huntin' for me.'

Wyeth made his humourless tight grin for the second time. 'You don't limp, Mister Malone, and you're not old enough nor built right. I'll know my man when I see him. He's neither you nor Josh Henley.'

'Then, if he was ever here in the canyon, most likely he's long gone.'

Wyeth's answer was a reflection of his bloodhound tenacity. 'This is where the trail came. Maybe he was here and left, but somewhere in Hell's Canyon there'll be someone who knew enough about him for me to keep tracking.' Wyeth hesitated, glanced around the store again and said, 'Have you ever considered selling out?'

Rufe made a short laugh. 'Never thought on it. I'm like you said, I can stay inside durin' hot weather an' fill the wood stove in winter.'

After the manhunter left, Rufe's opinion softened just a tad; Andrew Wyeth was human after all. That, or he was a damned good actor.

12

The Power of Gossip

In Hell's Canyon any variety of news spreads fast. Some of it, in fact probably two-thirds of it was manufactured by folks living in an isolated canyon and knew no other way to break boredom, but the arrival of the latest outsider and the questions he asked had aroused widespread and serious interest.

Rufe acknowledged having met Wyeth but declined to be drawn into a discussion of the man. Josh Henley who had fed the stranger and sat visiting with him was of the opinion Wyeth was in the canyon to buy a business or maybe some land.

It was the lack of genuine information fed by some pretty wild surmises that kept the interest high.

Folks knew Wyeth had visited Rufe's store; his business increased although he would say nothing except that Wyeth had asked if his store was for sale.

Wyeth was gone almost a week. Down in Angelina he worried Doctor Foster like a dog with a bone. Foster kept records, he said, going back to his first year in the Angelina country, but only on genuinely ill or injured people. He didn't write everything down. If someone needed a prescription for a back ache, lumbago, a sore throat or a particular pain he got paid for medicine and considered these cases too insignificant to record.

As for the Pinkerton man's questions and guarded answers, they were irritating to a man in his sixties who was set in his ways and disliked being badgered.

He reiterated what he had said at their first meeting; he had sold three bottles of laudanum to a grizzled older man who said he lived in Hell's Canyon and, when Andrew Wyeth described Josh Henley, the physician answered annoyedly, 'Sounds like the man. I don't remember; as I told you it was long ago and I don't believe I've seen him since. Yes, that sounds like him, Mister Wyeth.'

If Wyeth was anything he was thorough. Despite the lengthy lapse of time he talked to everyone he could find in the Angelina countryside who might remember an individual who limped and as with Doctor Foster when they did remember, it was invariably the wrong leg.

Wyeth's long absence inclined Rufe to suspect he had found a fresh trail and if it took him away from the canyon he would very likely never return.

There was no gossip to replace speculations about Wyeth so during his absence the stories were not only repeated but began gathering some interesting speculations, one of which maintained that Andrew Wyeth was an outlaw fugitive seeking an isolated area to hide out in.

Bert Freeman confided to Beulah during one of his rare visits to the settlement that Andrew Wyeth was really Frank James, Jesse James's brother.

Beulah, despite being sceptical about anything the unwashed old hermit said, had read some time back that when Jesse had been shot in the back and killed by a man named Robert Ford, that Frank James had afterwards dropped from sight, a fugitive with a bounty on his head.

Beulah passed her conjecture along until it became generally accepted. When Wyeth returned from Angelina and entered her eatery one chilly morning, Beulah's usual crankiness was in abeyance.

She served him a platter of ham and eggs, kept his coffee cup full and talked about the weather, the probability of a bad winter to come and when Wyeth arose, put coins on the counter and looked at her oddly, she carried the soiled dishes to the kitchen after Wyeth departed and told Maria Elena that as sure as she was standing there, Andrew Wyeth was Frank James.

When Maria Elena told Jim Elsworth what Beulah had said he carried the story to the store where Rufe listened without showing concern and eventually told Jim if the story was true he couldn't imagine a fugitive passing himself off as a Pinkerton detective. Fugitives wanted anonymity not notoriety.

Jim's response was delivered with a sly, narrow-eyed look. 'That's what I'd do. I'd swear I belonged to the right side of the law.'

Rufe was visited by Josh Henley one lukewarm autumn afternoon. Josh had heard the talk and adamantly denounced it. 'He's no more an outlaw than I am,' he told the storekeeper. 'Think on it, Rufe. If you was a fugitive would you ride into a community an' stir up interest askin' questions? Of course you wouldn't. An' somethin' else, Jesse wasn't tall an' had slitty eyes. His brother was taller an' didn't have slitty eyes.'

A couple of days later when Wyeth appeared in the store, he remarked on how differently folks treated him after his absence than they'd treated him before.

Rufe was blunt. 'They think you're Frank James, Jesse's brother.'

Wyeth went to the bench and sat down staring at Rufe. 'If that's a fact how did they come to that way of thinking?'

Rufe ignored the question. 'I remember hearin' there was a big reward on Jesse before he got killed ... I'm wonderin' if there's a reward out on his brother because if there is an' folks think you're Frank James, if I was you I'd grow an eye in the back of my head.'

Wyeth walked to the front of the store, stood there looking out. In an offhand way he said, 'Autumn's coming,' and slowly turned regarding Rufe. 'That was your chance. That's how Jess got killed, shot in the back.'

Rufe looked annoyed. 'I didn't say I believed you was Frank James.'

The lean man returned to the bench, groped for one of his expensive stogies, put it into his mouth without lighting it and regarded Rufe.

'Gossip,' he exclaimed. 'Every settlement like this one lives on it.'

Rufe neither agreed nor disagreed. He said, 'If I was in your fix I'd leave, or be gawd-awful careful. There's always folks lookin' for a way to get rich.'

Wyeth showed one of his dour little smiles. 'It's good advice, but I can't take it. Not yet anyway. Hell's Canyon is where the trail led me and until I'm satisfied Booth isn't here I got to search. Mister Malone, I need to find my man. You know everyone. I have an idea you could help. . . .'

'I told you about the only man with a limp I know of, Mister Wyeth. If you want a guess, I'd say wherever Booth is he isn't in Hell's Canyon.'

Wyeth's small smile lingered. 'If you're right, fine, but I can't just up and leave because you don't know my man. In fact, if I was a guessing man I'd say you know him. There's only this store for supplies in your canyon. Sooner or later I'd guess everyone passes through here. That's why I looked you up first.'

Jim Elsworth came in, saw Wyeth and hesitated for a moment before stiffly nodding and approaching the counter. 'I need four sets of cold rolled muleshoes,' he told Rufe whose answer was short. 'They're out back, Jim. Out where I keep all the heavy hardware.'

Rufe led the way, Jim followed. When they were on the loading dock out back, Elsworth looked over his shoulder and quietly said, 'He's settin' right there with a bounty on his head.'

Rufe pushed and pulled small kegs until he found the right one and as he picked out muleshoes one at a time he said, 'He's no more Frank James than I'm the Angel Gabriel. You got a forge? Shapin' these shoes proper'll need heat.'

Briefly, Jim was diverted. 'I been buildin' knot fires in a stone ring for years.'

'How about nails?'

'I got fours, sixes an' eights. Rufe?'

The storekeeper straightened up holding muleshoes in both hands. 'It's not true, Jim. Take my word for it.'

'Then who is he?'

'A Pinkerton detective.'

Elsworth took the plates and preceded Rufe back inside. The bench was empty; Andrew Wyeth had left the store. Jim put the shoes on the counter, pulled out a long leather purse, pushed up from the bottom, removed several coins and put them on the counter. He frowned while doing this and continued to frown when he looked up.

'We been friends a long time,' he said. 'What's he doin' here if he's a Pinkerton man?'

'I told you before, he's huntin' a man with a limp. Ask him, Jim. He'll tell you. Maybe you can help him.' Rufe also said, 'I think he's wastin' his time but he's one of them gents like a bird dog. It'll be a cold day in Hell before he quits.'

'Beulah says—'

'You already told me what she says.'

'An' you know better?'

'Jim, look him up, talk to him.'

'You're satisfied he's not Frank James?'

'Yes.'

Elsworth picked up the muleshoes and started for the door as he said, 'That's good enough for me. He ain't Frank James.'

The following morning early, shortly after Rufe had unlocked the roadway door, Andrew Wyeth walked in. He acted no differently than he usually acted but when he spoke there was an edge to his words.

'Mister Malone, how long have you known a man named Bert Freeman?'

Rufe looked incredulously at the other man. 'Not him, Mister Wyeth. He's a harmless old man who lives in a filthy shack up a spur canyon. How long? I'd say about twelve, fourteen years.'

'He limps?'

'Not that I ever noticed. He's old, walks like it an' acts like it. He walks sort of like a crab. What's known about him is that he laughs and grins like a magpie. As far back as I can remember he's always struck me as bein' a man born with one foot out of the stirrups.' Rufe leaned on the counter regarding Wyeth sceptically. 'You think he's your man?'

'He uses laudanum. On a ride out yonder I came on to some boys named Houston. Freeman's place is about a mile from their yard up a small draw. They told me they knew the old man fairly well, that he walks bent over.'

'I could've told you that. He's old.'

Wyeth ignored the interruption. 'They told me when he straightens up he favours one leg.'

Rufe continued to regard the Pinkerton detective sceptically. As far back as Rufe remembered, Bert Freeman had always walked stooped. He attributed it to old age. He'd seen his share of old men who walked like that, some used canes some didn't.

Wyeth caught Rufe's interest when he said, 'He gets the Houstons to fetch supplies from down at Angelina. They told me every trip they bring back bottles of laudanum. You know him pretty well; does he carry a gun?'

'Not that I've ever noticed. He's likely got guns, livin' up where he lives a man'd be a fool not to have guns handy. Cougar, bears and whatnot prowl that part of the canyon.' Rufe had a question. 'How old was Booth when he shot the president?'

'Twenty-three.'

Rufe did some rough figuring before speaking again. 'Bert Freeman's got to be in his seventies.'

Wyeth nodded. 'Figure the difference between when the president got shot and now. It'll come out close.'

Rufe straightened up off the counter. 'Did you scout up his place?'

'Not close but I followed directions and found it. There's an old tumbledown corral with a horse in it. There's some chickens and a goat, most likely a milk goat. It's about the filthiest, unkempt, rundown place I've ever seen.'

Rufe shrugged about that as he said, 'Those old gaffers live like boar bears.'

Wyeth accepted that without comment. 'Mister Malone, that's a perfect hideout.'

Rufe's answer to that was candid. 'That kind of country is free for the settlin'. There's other places like that in the canyon.'

Wyeth arose from the bench. 'Right or wrong I've got to make sure. It's the only other lead I've got since coming here.'

Rufe watched the lanky man leave the store, wagged his head and went after the feather duster. One advantage to the arrival of cold weather and snow was that dust wouldn't come in.

It was about mid-afternoon when he got a shock. Bert Freeman came in grinning from ear to ear. Out front his old saddle animal dozed at the tie rack.

Freeman had shaved recently but not very well. His hair had been shorn too, by unsteady hands holding dull shears. The second part of Rufe's surprise was that Freeman was attired in clean and patched britches and shirt.

The moment the bent old man began to speak Rufe knew what was coming. Freeman's voice was a pitiful whine. He said if Rufe would trust him he'd pay the next time he found nuggets, which was what he had been saying for a long time. Rufe took the nearly illegible list and went among the shelves reaching for the listed items. When he put them on the counter, Freeman's perpetual smile widened. His purchases were things such as salt, sugar and baking powder which could not be grown in a garden.

Rufe asked if the old man was feeling well and got a quizzical look. 'Feelin' as good as I can. Why: do I look puny?'

'You look fine,' Rufe replied, 'it's just a common thing to say. Bert. . . .'

'Yes.'

'You'n the Houstons visit now an' then?'

'Not real often. But yestiddy one of 'em rode close. I saw him from a distance, couldn't make out which one it was.' Freeman's smile returned. 'Good neighbours, Mister Malone. A man needs good neighbours. I'd best be gettin' on home. Thank you. I'll come back as soon as I find some nuggets.'

For the second time this day Rufe watched a man leave his store. He might have had time to wonder about the rider the old man had seen and thought it was one of the Houstons if another customer hadn't arrived. This time it was the squinty-eyed, cranky widow-woman and her purpose was not to buy it was to inform Rufe in a lowered voice that the stranger she had seen visit the store was, her voice dropped to almost a whisper, Frank James, brother to the outlaw Jesse James.

She reared back squinting harder than ever wait-

ing for the astonishment she expected. Rufe
humoured her. 'I'll be damned.'

'I seen him come in here several times. Did he use
his real name?'

'He said his name was Andrew Wyeth, that he's a
Pinkerton detective.'

The old woman beamed. 'You see? Them kind'll
lie when the truth'll fit better. I was wonderin', do
you expect there's bounty money for him?'

Rufe replied forthrightly. 'If there is I'd advise folks
not to try'n collect it. Them James boys got a reputation for shootin' first an' enquirin' afterwards.'

The old woman nodded. 'That may be, but sure as
I'm standin' here someone'll try. Good day to you,
Mister Malone.'

Rufe watched another visitor depart. This time
wondering if his latest customer owned a gun and if
she would be foolish enough to use it.

Knowingly or not, Andrew Wyeth was being set up
as a target. He didn't worry about the Pinkerton man
getting caught nosing around Bert Freeman's place.
Wyeth had left town hours before old Bert had
ridden in.

There were three other customers, all settlement
folks which made it impossible for Rufe to visit
Elsworth's wagon camp until late afternoon.

Jim was rumpled, soiled and sitting in wagon
shade sweating. When Rufe appeared Jim looked up
and said, 'I been shoein' all four in one day for years.
Today I shod two an' had to rest.'

Rufe was not tactful when he said, 'Old age, Jim,'
and also sat in the shade while Elsworth mopped off
sweat and unhappily eyed the two mules still to be
shod.

Rufe eyed them too. 'It can wait until tomorrow,' he said.

Elsworth was slow to reply. 'I'd like to pull out tomorrow.' He faced his old friend. 'I won't be leavin' alone.'

Rufe picked up a sliver, dug out his clasp knife and whittled. 'Maria Elena?'

'Yes. We'll trail up to Zephyr to get married. She didn't want to get hitched down in Angelina where folks might recognize her.'

'Does Beulah know, Jim?'

'She's goin' to tell her, then roll her belongings and come to the camp. That's why I'd like to get them other two critters shod, so we can leave the canyon early before Beulah comes along to raise hell.'

Rufe stood up. 'I'll help you. While you're restin' I'll do the trimming.'

13

'Good Luck'

Shoeing mules is a sight different from shoeing horses, which have round feet. Mule hooves are narrower and elongated. Also, as in this instance, their feet were like iron from a long summer on dry hard earth.

Rufe finished trimming the second mule, which was the eldest and had a nasty trick; when a shoer was bent over, the old mule would bite his rump. Rufe yelled at Jim, who was sound asleep in the shade and came awake with a pounding heart.

'The old son of a bitch bit me.'

'Oh, I should've told you. I tie his head around on the opposite side so he can't do that.'

'Where's the rasp?'

Jim stood up. 'Nobody hits my mules, Rufe. It's just a game with him. He's old and don't have no real bad habits. Here, I'll finish.'

Rufe went to sit in the shade, flinched and eased around to perch on the unbitten cheek. 'I'd shoot that old bastard.'

'No, you wouldn't. He's as honest as the day is long . . . I named him after you.' Elsworth straightened up from rasping.

'Rufe, you hadn't ought to bite folks. I've told you that a hunnert times. Rufe! You do that again, I'll slap you!'

The old mule looked straight ahead.

As Elsworth picked up the foot again he said, 'You ever been in Texas?'

Rufe moved gingerly. 'Been through part of it. Why, is that where you'n Maria Elena are going?'

'That's where she wants to go. She's got a sister down there. She told me she don't speak English.' Jim dropped the rasp, placed a shoe for fit and picked up his hammer. He already had two nails in his mouth as he spoke. 'I think we'll go north, up among the tradin' an' freightin' settlements.'

A lanky, rumpled man appeared from in front of the wagon. Jim had his back turned and didn't see him but Rufe did and nodded.

Andrew Wyeth eased down on an old leather *alforja*, fished wordlessly in a pocket, brought forth an old small pistol as he said, 'That's the right serial number.'

When Rufe took the pistol to examine he said, 'The right number for what?'

'The pistol John Booth shot President Lincoln with.'

Rufe continued examining the gun for a long moment before handing it back as he said, 'Old Bert Freeman?'

Wyeth didn't pocket the pistol, he held it gently. 'Your friend was the assassin.'

Rufe looked out where Elsworth was labouring over the second shoe. 'Where's Bert?' he asked quietly.

Wyeth relaxed against the wagon. 'I'll tell you what

happened,' he said, also gazing out where the freighter was bent over with his back to them. 'Someday I'll figure out how he did it. I expect he's been maybe expecting someone like me to ride into his gully. Anyway, he let me dismount, didn't say a word, whipped out that old pistol and fired.'

'He missed?'

'It misfired. You saw it; I'd say that old gun and its loads have been lying somewhere where rust fused things. I tried to punch out the casing and couldn't budge it.

'He yelled like a crazy man, ran at me and fired again. That time the old gun went off like a cannon. He was running and I was sidling.'

When Wyeth paused this time, Rufe continued to look out where Jim Elsworth was rasping nail ends as he said, 'You shot him?'

'Yes . . . afterwards I ransacked the shack, found the numbers on the gun and some newspapers so old they was hard to read. Six of them all about the assassination. Found some other things; a picture of a young woman. On the back was a date and some scribbling. It said, "When the red legs got through with her she died" and another date.'

Rufe picked up his whittling stick dug out his knife and went to whittling. Wyeth stood up saying he had to care for his horse and walked around the wagon out of sight.

Rufe was still sitting and whittling when Jim came over, dropped down where Wyeth had sat, used a soiled sleeve to mop off sweat as he said, 'Ready now. If you see Beulah I'd take it kindly if you wouldn't say anythin'. We'll pull out before sunrise.'

Rufe stood up, pocketed his knife, patted Jim on

the shoulder and said, 'Good luck.'

Elsworth watched him walking away. He'd never heard Rufe's voice in that tone before. He told himself it was because Rufe was saddened over the excellent probability that they would never see each other again. They wouldn't.

The following morning with the sun climbing, Rufe saddled up for the ride to the Freeman place. He didn't take a shovel, old Bert had several.

As he was riding out, Beulah emerged from the eatery and said, 'She's gone!'

Rufe nodded and didn't look back. He had never liked seeing women cry.

By the time he got to Freeman's gully the sun was high. Old Bert was lying face down where he'd died. Blue-tailed flies were already gathering. A goat bleated and the old horse looked pitifully from his corral. Rufe turned them both out before hunting for the shovel.

Oddly enough, old Bert's canyon had good soil. Even so, digging the grave required several hours. After burying the old man and mounding the grave Rufe groped among odds and ends until he found something suitable. With dusk approaching, he made the cross, scratched Bert's name on it and used the flat side of a shovel to drive the marker into the ground.

He rode back the way he had come, sore and aching. Digging holes in the ground required the use of bones and muscles storekeepers rarely had occasion to use.

It was almost dark by the time he rode past Beulah's place on his way to put up the horse. She may have heard him passing or just as likely was standing in the eatery doorway; whatever the reason, she saw him, called softly and, when he drew rein, she walked over and said, 'She could've said she was leaving.'

Rufe looked down. 'Beulah, you'd've raised hell. My guess is she didn't want to remember the last meeting between you two was in an argument.'

'I'll miss her somethin' terrible.'

Rufe did not share that feeling but he said, 'We did what we could do. Folks can only protect friends so far. When they leave,' he shrugged, 'we got the satisfaction that we did the best we could do for 'em. After they leave they go out of our lives.'

Beulah's eyes welled with unshed tears. 'She was like a daughter to me, Rufe.'

He knew that and said something he didn't believe but which turned out to be the truth. 'She'll never forget you, Beulah. Someday maybe she'll come back. Now I got to take care of the horse.'

Maria Elena never returned. As with Jim Elsworth, she had her own life to live and it did not include coming back to Hell's Canyon.